MW01600904

I dedicate this book to my fallen
Angels: Willie 'Frank' Hopson,
Lovely Hopson, Joseph 'Jay Banga'
Owens, Kevin 'Reddot' Davis and
Silas 'The Stylist' Brown A.I.P

I also dedicate this book to my
children, Kha'Lani & Ayden; the
Ashland Ave Gang (this is for y'all).
Thank you all for walking with me
through my darkest times. A's up or
K's up, till my day's up.

CHAPTER 1

The first thing that I saw when I regained consciousness was my grandfather, Pop, or Frank to his associates, choking the life out of a police officer.

"What in your right mind would make you put your hands on a ten year old child?" Pop asked.

Hoarsely the officer responded, "What's it to you Frank? This little fucker needs to learn some respect."

"And just who the hell are you to decide who needs to be taught or giving lessons on respect?"

I gathered myself and made it to my feet. "I'm ok, Pop, let's just go home."

The officer realized that he picked the wrong kid and his eyes widened to the size of grapefruits.

Pop tightened his jaw. "No, you're going to tell me exactly why a lawman that's sworn to protect and serve would decide to hit you over the head with his billy club. And I mean it now!" he shouted.

"It's nothing, Pop, really," I insisted.

Pop was having none of that. "I mean now dammit!"

I knew Pop was seriously agitated because he never shouted. He was too reticent.

"I was walking to the store when he pulled up and threw me against his car. He asked me my name and I told him they call me G.I. Joe, then he told me that was a stupid name to have. So I told him that his face was a stupid one to have."

I almost burst out laughing but I knew Pop wasn't for the playing so I continued. "I told him they call me that because my grandpa used to be an Army man. Then he asked me if that was what I wanted to be when I grew up. I said no, I wanna be just like Pablo Escobar. That's when I got hit over the head."

Pop finally let Officer Billy Club go.

"Frank, I'm really sorry. I didn't know this was one of your grandchildren!" At that point, you could see that he was extremely petrified and sweating profusely.

It seemed like an eternity, but when Pop finally spoke, you could tell that he meant business. "If I ever see you or even hear about you putting your hands on one of these kids, I'll skin you alive. Now get from round here while you still have life left in you!"

Officer Billy Club tripped over his bumper and fell face first into the street, nearly getting run over by a passing car, while attempting to flee.

Pop and I went into the backyard and he told me to go get some rest, because at 4AM he was going to teach me how to fend for myself.

I don't think I've ever ran so fast to my room without my mom chasing me with a belt. Pop was finally going to show me those infamous defensive close combat moves he's always talking about. I ate two

Benadryl tablets because I knew I would die of anticipation before I would be able to fall asleep.

Boy was I in for a rude awakening.

At four, Pop woke me and my younger brother, Eyes, up and told us to get dressed and meet him at the truck in twenty minutes.

An hour later we were sitting on the bank of the Mississippi River with fishing lines cast out. My little brother had a dumb ass grin on his face while I was sitting there mad as hell. I was so mad that I started throwing rocks at the river to try to hurt it. After I realized what I was doing, I burst out laughing.

"I thought you were going to teach us how to fend for ourselves, Pop?" I mumbled just loud enough for him to catch.

"You don't think feeding yourself is fending for oneself?" he asked pointedly.

"Well, I guess you're right. So Pop, why was that officer so scared of you yesterday? Any other person would have been dead or in jail within a blink of an eye."

"Before you were born, I was one of the most notable figures in the community and one of the most feared. Even some civil rights clubs were trying to recruit me. There were very few people that would go toe to toe with your grandfather in his heyday," Pop said, referring to himself in third person.

My brother was so quiet that I forgot he was there. He suddenly started screaming.

Pop and I looked back and he was being pulled towards the river. He had a big fish on the line, Pop helped him reel in the fish. In total we caught seven nice sized channel catfish and headed home.

When we got home, Eyes and I saw our friends out throwing the football around. We knew they were waiting on us because Saturday was the day that we would go to different neighborhoods to play sandlot football. Our team was the Ashland

Avenue Gangstas or AAG for short. I think people let us win because the first time we lost, we had an all out brawl and none of us even had a scratch on us.

Pop knew we were itching to go play but not that day. "You boys go in the backyard and I'll be there behind you. When we get done, I'll bake y'all a sweet potato pie and let y'all split one of my peach Vess," he bribed since he knew we couldn't resist his pie or peach sodas.

By the end of the day we were full of pie and soda plus we knew how to catch fish, skin and clean them to be cooked.

When Pop sent us to bed I asked him, "Pop why or what made you so powerful back in the day, and why did you stop?"

"Well I stopped because you were born, son. The other stuff isn't important, some things are better left where they are at."

CHAPTER 2

"Let me help you with your tie, it's crooked," Pop said while helping me with my appearance an hour before my high school graduation. He was more excited than I was.

"Your mother told me that you're graduating at the top of your class and you have a bunch of full ride scholarship offers for football. I want you to know that I'm extremely proud of you, growing up in this neighborhood. Many of the kids often will not make it out. Have you decided what college you're going to attend?"

"No sir, I've visited all of them and I'm torn between Michigan and USC. Besides it's just college, Pop, why are you getting all mushy like I'm about to die or something?" I asked with a playful smirk on my face.

"Only if you knew the sacrifices that were made when you were born. I want nothing but the best for you, that's why I raised you up as my son instead of my grandchild. Your mom fought me day in and day out up until the second you were introduced to the world. She never wanted me to leave behind my life in the military, but I couldn't allow my only daughter to raise a child on her own. I feel responsible for your father going to jail. If it weren't for me he wouldn't have been in that situation. When you get into the league, you can take my position and carry the family."

"It's not like you were rolling in dough while you were in the service, Pop. Besides, why would you feel like you're responsible for him going to jail? He was selling drugs, what does that have to do with you and the Army?" I was genuinely confused. By the look on Pop's face, I knew that this conversation was nearing an end.

"Some things that I've done in the past, I will go through great depths to protect this family from," he answered as he patted my shoulders and giving me a satisfied look-over.

"Now that's how a young man is supposed to present himself. Now go walk across that stage like a Khrist is supposed to before I skin you alive.

***

After graduation, those of us from the hood that graduated that night talked our families into taking us to KOBE's Steakhouse in Maryland Heights, a St. Louis municipality. You can tell by the name of the town that our parents couldn't afford to take us there, but somehow, some way they pulled it off. KOBE's is one of those hibachi restaurants that has a grill in the middle of the table and you watch a chef put on a show while he cooks.

Sometimes things just seem to be going too well, tonight was one of those nights. After a great dinner with nothing but fun and laughs, my homie's, Stuck's father brought up college again and future plans. He went around the table asking everyone where they would be attending.

I instantly started sweating. Remember that sandlot football team, Ashland Avenue Gangstas? Well over the years we became a real gang, hey, it happens, and my friends knew I was not ready to answer that question. Everyone except my high school sweetheart, Tanner.

Stuck took the lead so that I'd be the last to have to answer. "I'm going to go to Ranken Tech."

Lazy: Missouri Western
Sanchez: Lincoln University
Fatt Rell: Robert Morris
Shoota: Mizzou
Tanner: Harris Stowe

And last but not least, the eyes fell upon yours truly. "I'm not ready to commit to a college yet, plus, I have a couple of weeks to think it all the way through."

I can tell that all the adults, and Tanner, were disappointed in my answer because they just stared at me.

"What, do I have a booger in my nose or something?" I asked, trying to break the tension.

On the ride home none of my family seemed upset but they still didn't talk to me.

When we pulled up to the house, Tanner was already sitting on the porch with her arms folded.

I knew I was in for it.

Pop tossed me the keys to his Chevy Beretta and wished me luck.

As I walked up to her, I saw her lips forming insulting words but I cut her off by stealing a kiss. When we finally freed our mouths she had tears in her eyes.

I shook my head. "Not here, Love."

"Then where, because we're going to discuss this, tonight," she challenged pointedly.

"Well me and the guys were talking about all driving down to the riverfront for a few hours," I answered while heading to open the passenger door so that she could climb in.

Once we got to the riverfront, we parked the cars so that we faced the Arch and sat on the hoods of them.

Lazy popped a bottle of Hennessy. He poured me twice as much and said, "You're gonna need it."

Tanner stared at me until I finally spoke.

"Baby Love, I want you to hear me out before you blow your shit. I absolutely love football and I enjoy playing it, but it doesn't make me happy. Besides, people like me don't make it to the pros."

"That's some bullshit and you know it, Keefer. So what makes you happy, and what do you plan on doing? Whatever it is, you're leaving Ashland! I know you love the block but the block doesn't love you back. For the last four years, I've sat back and watched you go through brawls, riots, stabbings and shootings. I've lost count how many nights I thought you weren't going to come knocking on my window so we could sleep together until it was time for you to sneak out before my parents woke."

"Damn, I know you love me and all but quit trying to be my mama. I have a plan, I'm just afraid to tell my mom and grandpa. They want me to play ball so bad, but over the years, I fell in love with being behind the gun."

She interrupted me before I could finish, "If you say you can't leave so you can stay here and be a gangster, yo ass won't have to worry about them niggas from Lex Ave killing you, because I'll shoot you right here right now. I dare you to try me," Tanner challenged tersely.

Boy was she sexy when she threatened me, all five feet, one hundred twenty six pounds of her.

Mockingly I looked dead in her face and said with an even tone, "I can't leave so I can stay here and be a gangster." Before she could swing on me, I hurried up and started laughing, "No seriously, when those recruiters came to the school a few months ago, I enlisted in the Army. Before you get to trippin', we are out here shooting and killing for free, so why not go and get paid for it? I'm good at this shit and next to getting behind that big ol' wagon that you're draggin' that's the best thrill that I've experienced."

"Why in the hell would they be mad at you for joining the military? I personally think that's a wonderful idea, the reasoning is stupid but I support you one hundred percent."

A rush of relief fell over me. "I don't know, Pop used to be in the Army before I was born and for some odd reason he left it to quote unquote protect us. I know he's going to shit a brick when I tell them."

"I think you should just tell them straight up. And since you mentioned this wagon," she turned around and made it clap for me.

"Mom booked me a room for tonight, and if you promise to break the news to them tomorrow, I'll let you put an x-pill in my booty hole," Tanner teased.

My mouth instantly watered because I knew what was in store for the night. "You're a nasty lil' bitch."

"My pussy gets so wet up when you talk dirty to me," she said while biting down on her bottom lip.

Chapter 3

After an exhausting night with Tanner, I had to own up to my side of the bargain. She wanted to be present to help me get through it, but I told her that was something that I would have to handle on my own. She didn't like being left out but she eventually submitted to my request.

I asked Pop to make fish and spaghetti for dinner so that I could announce my decision. I knew fish was his favorite food and I needed something to keep him occupied while I made my announcement.

At dinner it was barely room to walk in the dining room. I felt smothered but I had to get this over with, the quicker the better.

I quieted everyone down and jumped straight in. "Thank you all for coming out to hear my decision on college. I guess I'll make this short and sweet. I, Keefer Khrist, am choosing to go to boot camp."

Confused faces spread like wildfires throughout the dining room. However, I noticed Pop tense up, he knew exactly what I meant.

My mom on the other hand didn't. "What kind of school names itself Boot Camp, and where exactly is this campus?"

As Pop pushed away from the table he had the stare of death locked in on me. As he exited the room he said, " The dummy means he's going to the Army, Chelle."

It was so quiet that you could hear the ghost of the house stealing food off the dining room table until my mom started crying and faked a faint. Her boyfriend, Fox, helped her up and carried her out of the room. Everybody else just stood there exchanging looks. It was even more quiet now, I could have sworn I heard the rats and the roaches in the walls playing rock paper scissors to see who would be the first to run out and steal the crumbs off of the floor.

After all of the visitors left, there was so much tension in the house that you could cut it with a guillotine, without the blade. I needed out.

Like I did any other time I needed to get my mind right, I went and knocked on Tanner's window, don't ask me why I always snuck in during the day, I guess it made the mood more spontaneous.

"So how'd it go, Red Face? You want me to kill them now or later?"

"You know I hate that pet name," I said as I cringed. "However, I knocked them dead, literally. My mom fainted, Pop called me dumb and hasn't said anything to me since, oh and I think he legally changed my name to, Stupid. Everyone else just stared at me like I had on a helmet and was having a full course meal of crayons. Other than that it went swell darling," I said darling with an English accent.

Now it was time for us to have our 'talk'.

CHAPTER 4

Tanner's mom poked her head through the door. "Oh, hi son-in-law, I didn't even hear you come through the front door."

I whispered in a stealthy voice, "That's because I'm a ninja."

She just stared at me then spoke to Tanner. "Your boyfriend is weird, you sure know how to pick them. Dinner's almost ready, tell the invisible ninja that he's welcome to join us as long as he leaves the nunchucks here," she said as she closed the door.

I turned to Tanner. "Soooo, that wasn't funny?"

"No bro, that was lame as hell," she said, rolling her eyes.

"I told you not to call me bro, it seems creepy and incestuous," I said sternly.

"Ok, but you think daddy doesn't seem the same? That's probably worse."

"That shit played out anyway, call me Sir Daddy Dragon Master," I said, striking a superhero pose.

"Where. Thee. Fuck. Did. That. Come. From?" Tanner asked sourly.

"Well you like calling me daddy so I just added sir to that, and I'm a master of the wagon you draggin'. Get it Sir Daddy Dragon Master."

"Yea, it's a no for me. My mom is right, my boyfriend is weird. So when do you leave for the Army?"

"Well that's actually what I came over to talk to you about. I'm so glad I'm not the only person in this relationship with super powers. I love you even more now. But I leave a week after my birthday in September. I know that I'll be going to boot camp and AIT, which is the training that I'll have to do for my job that I'll be doing while serving…"

She cut me off mid sentence, "You're rambling as well as stalling, get to the point!"

Shit, I didn't know if it was just me or it was getting hot in her room.

"Ok, so I don't know where they're going to station me when I graduate AIT and I don't want you to feel obligated to wait on me. College might open new doors for you and I don't want to hold you back from that."

"Nigga, did you just break up with me?" Tanner asked, balling up her fist.

"Um, no. Tan I just gave you the out to break up with me. I know the stuff that college women do and I want you to enjoy yourself. Besides, I don't know when I'll be able to come visit."

"You're not getting rid of me that easily, sweet cheeks," she slapped me on the ass, which she knew that I hate with a passion. "The only man for my eyes would be you, and after a semester, I might be able to transfer my credits to a college near the base that you'll be assigned to."

"Are you sure, Tan, because I'm the crazy type of boyfriend. If I catch you cheating on me, I'm going to wait until y'all are fast asleep and then flip the mattress. Then I'll super glue your eyes open so you'll be forced to watch me torture him to death."

"Sounds sexy, but yes I'm sure. I'll even put a nanny cam in my room and you can creep on me at any time you feel necessary. Better yet, give me your phone, there's an app that allows you to see my location and to turn my camera on at your discretion."

"Wow, I just went from a superhero to a peeping Tom within a matter of minutes. Wait, so will you be able to do that to my phone too?"

"I mean if that's a problem, we could always cut off your dick and leave it here with me," she said while rubbing my piece through my pants.

I gulped. "How long did you say it took for this app to download?"

"Yeah, I thought you'd see it my way."

CHAPTER 5

It was the day before I was set to leave for boot camp. Over the summer Pop finally started saying more than two words to me. He now said three, "You're fucking stupid."

My mom finally stopped fainting when someone said, Army.

The AAG gang and I went on a few farewell missions. We stepped on the Lex for three weeks straight. I think they had an addiction to lead.

Tanner and I had so much sex, I thought my penis was going to be permanently embedded inside of her. We were doing the nasty two to three times a day. Her mom walked in on us once and I had my meat jammed down her throat while she was hanging backwards off of the bed. She screamed "Get that out of her," slammed the door and kept repeating, "My baby is a whore."

Yea I wasn't invited to any more dinners after that.

I was the last member of the AAG graduating class to leave for my future endeavors. That was my last night being a ghost in the house. I was tired of trying to walk through walls anyway. Whoever said ghosts can go through solid objects was a damn lie, that myth is not plausible. I figured I would give it one more attempt before I jumped from the bird's nest.

Pop called me just as I was about to hit full speed. "Come in here for a second. And walk through the doorway, I'm sure the walls have filled out enough reports of assault charges on you."

"Twenty two words, woah that's a record, Pop, what's up?" I joked.

He shook his head. "Just fucking stupid. There, is that better? Have a seat, I need to get this off of my chest. First, I'm against this decision that you made and it broke my heart to hear that you're actually going to follow through with it. However, you're an adult now and being an adult is about making choices. I just wish you would have come and talked to me first. I don't like it but I have to respect it, you're grown now. Remember to always be safe, keep your head down and on a swivel. Find you somebody that'll watch your six like you'll watch theirs. That's the best advice that I can give you, if you have any questions, ever, don't hesitate to call me. No matter the time, I'll always answer. I love you, soldier now come give the old man a hug."

"Still not going to tell me about your time in the service, are you?"

"Not a chance."

After Pop stopped being sentimental, my dad called from prison to wish me luck. He told me to be safe and he's sorry he couldn't be here to see me off. And something about sending him some pictures of some military bikini women, whatever that might be.

At 5AM, my mom's boyfriend, Fox, took me to the airport because my mom fainted again and Pop said he couldn't watch me walk off to the one place he dreaded the most. I guess he already saw me as being dead.

Fort Jackson, here I come.

CHAPTER 6

The first three weeks of boot camp were complete hell. Day one they shaved all of us bald and screamed/spat in our faces for hours. I think our drill sergeants were half human half Rottweilers.

Then we exercised so much as if we were training to be bodybuilders. Every time somebody messed up we were put in the front leaning rest position, that's military jargon for the starting push-up position. When we heard, "half right face," we knew it was time to try to push the earth out of orbit.

That was the entire three weeks; sleep, eat, formation, exercise, safety classes, spit showers, exercise, formation, spit showers, exercise, eat, sleep and finally repeat; six days a week. I started receiving grievances from my arms, threatening to run away.

Our drill sergeants promised us if we made it through the first three weeks, then on that Sunday they would take us to the beach. The whole company exploded with cheers.

Dumb ass privates. For those of you enlisting in the military, if you ever hear you're going to the beach, DO NOT GO, I repeat DO NOT GO! It's a trick. Go to sick call that day. The beach is a football field sized sand pit and they make you ranger crawl back and forth until you puke. Then they make you do it some more.

After we completed the first three weeks, they eased up on the exercising and started training us to be soldiers. By the start of the fourth week, I knew how to sleep standing up until somebody called out "at ease" for the Non-commissioned Officers or "attention" for the Commissioned Officers. We took turns going on watch so the rest could get their cow nap on. The exercises weren't as hard anymore and I learned how to eat full course meals in two minutes.

Over the next three weeks we went through extraneous weapons training. Everything from dismantling, cleaning, reassembling, firing and proper storage. We learned how to operate over ten different weapons and six different explosive devices. During zeroing day, where you had to line your weapon sights with your eyesight, I was the first to properly zero my weapon.

That was a bad idea, the drill sergeants started expecting the best from me and pushed me harder than the rest of the platoon.

When Thanksgiving rolled around, we were given our phones and were allowed to contact our families. As soon as I turned my phone on, my phone dinged multiple times back to back. The voicemail box was full and I had over three hundred new text messages, two hundred of the texts were pictures and words of encouragement from Tanner. She also had more than half of my voicemails.

I figured it would be best to FaceTime her first.

She answered on the first ring. "I was wondering how long it was going to take you to return a phone call or something," she joked.

"Well hello to you too, my Baby Love, I just turned my phone on, sheesh," I responded submissively.

"I know exactly how long your phone has been turned on. Remember that app that I installed on your phone? It notifies me as soon as it is powered back up, it also sends a picture of the person turning it on in case of theft."

"God, that's creepy," I said as chills ran down my spine.

"Not as creepy as you look with a naked head and face. Do me a favor, until your hair grows back, stay away from elementary school," she jabbed, twisting her face up.

"Hardy har har, aren't you a real funny guy."

"Oh don't be such a wuss. So how's basic training coming along? I was thinking about coming up to visit for Christmas break."

"It's going rather well, I can sleep standing up, win a chicken eating contest, clean and shoot a gun in my sleep and I'm so used to exercising, I can do a push-up with my eyeballs. But coming here won't be necessary, boo, they give us leave for Christmas and the New Year, so I'll be coming home for a few weeks."

"Well that saves me some time and money. I'll book us a room for those weeks, I'm going to need all the time I can get with you. By the way, did you get the pics I sent of my new toy?"

"Yes, I got it and I heard it in the background of the voicemails you left me moaning and screaming my name."

"I knew you'd get a kick out of those. This thing makes me squirt so much, I was going to send you a video of that but I'd rather show you in person."

"When I first heard you moaning, I almost lost my shit. I thought you pocket dialed me while you were fucking, then I heard the buzzing and you started calling out my name. Yea, I thought I was going to have to murder someone's dog."

She started laughing. "No babe, I've stayed true to my word. By the way, I don't have to come there and kill anyone, do I?"

"No my love, you don't. But there is one drill sergeant that found out that I was from St. Louis with golds in my mouth, and every time she sees me, she starts singing that song Grillz by Nelly."

"I'll be there tonight."

I could hear her breathing heavily through the phone, so I started laughing. "Sheesh, I'm really wearing off on you. Chill boo, I wouldn't cross that boundary."

She was still pissed so I swung for the fences. "Sooooo… I know this is kind of out of tradition but will you marry me?"

"Now why would you want to do that Red Face?"

"Woman, I knew I was going to marry you the first day I met your parents. You gave me a handjob at the dinner table while they were sitting right across from us. It took everything in me to keep my composure. I'm pretty sure my kids are still plastered under their kitchen table."

"Nope, I scooped them off when you were done and ate them with my meal," Tanner teased.

"You're a murderer," I joked back.

"And proud. So is that all, you only want to marry me for sexual reasons?"

"No, that's not all. You appeal to all of my senses, everything just goes haywire when you get within twenty feet of me. You're just as spontaneous as I am, you're intelligent, you push me to be the best version of myself. You're supportive, whatever I go through you don't judge and you guide me when I'm blind. Oh, I forgot to mention that wagon that you're draggin', and last but certainly not least, I love the hell out of you. I want to grow old and gray with you."

"And why couldn't you propose to me in person?"

"That would be because I don't think I'll be out of you long enough to ask any questions."

"You can't be serious," she said with an aggravated tone.

"You want seriousness? Well let's get serious, I want to marry you when I come home for Christmas exodus. I'll send you my card information so you can pay for any deposits and once I complete basic training, I'll get ten thousand of my sign on bonus. Whatever balances are left, I'll pay out of that."

Drumroll, and cue the tears.

"Yes, yes, yes. Oh my God. Red Face, yes I'll marry you. There's so much that I have to do. I'll call you later, love you."

Just like that, she was gone as quick as she came.

I FaceTimed my mom, she was on the verge of fainting again. Pop said he was ready for me to come home. My brother Eyes told me that he had dropped out and my sister was suspended until further notice for inciting a riot in the lunchroom.

Yep things were just peachy.

The guys from the block and I had an hour long conference call. I told them about boot camp and my plan on marrying Tanner. They argued over who was going to be the best man and that I had to decide who plays that role. I told them that they all would get to play their share of best man, my wedding would be the first wedding without groomsmen and a list full of best men.

Over the weekend I only heard from Tanner a handful of times.

Three times to ask me for my invite list, grooms list, color options, catering options and who to talk to if she needed to direct the grooms for tuxedo fittings. Twice to have phone sex, that rose toy really knew how to treat a woman.

I told her to contact Lazy, he's my best man, but not to tell him that because they'll start fighting each other over that spot.

Thanksgiving weekend finally over, it was time to get back to work. Over the next month we were in the field doing field operations and training.

They took us to the gas chamber, which is a big room that they filled with tear gas. As soon as the gas fills the room they make you remove your gas mask and state your name, social security number, birthday and recite the Soldier's Creed.

Impossible!

By the time you're midway through your social, you're choking and gagging. If you tried to run, they slammed you and held you down longer. Good thing I blew my nose real good, because if I hadn't, there would be boogers all over the instructor's face. Then they make you walk out still coughing and choking but tell you to wave your arms at your side to keep from rubbing your eyes, which made us look like we were flapping chickens exiting a chicken coop. Then they tase you as soon as you exit the door. Not only were my eyes burning, I had wet pants. Talk about embarrassing.

We learned how to shoot from the back of moving vehicles, day and night.

We repelled down a thirty foot wall and out of a helicopter.

We had to crawl through a mud pit that had razor wire two feet high at night while there was live fire a foot above that. I had to fight the urge to stand up and see if the rounds were real.

We slept in 20 man tents in sleeping bags, and sometimes at

night our drill sergeants would throw flashbangs or pepper spray grenades inside while we were sleeping. I had to start sleeping fully dressed with my gas mask on, just in case, talk about the most uncomfortable sleep ever.

We learned how to warm up meals ready to eat(MRE) in the provided bag with hand warmers. On accident I dropped some of the hot rocks in a water bottle and closed it and the bottle exploded. I was in the front leaning rest position for two hours in the snow. So not fun.

They taught us to navigate with only a compass. Well I thought they taught us because without my team, I would have been lost.

We learned about combat life saving. That consisted of CPR, how to field dress wounds properly, tie tourniquets, how to insert IVs and how to call in medical evacuations with situation reports(SitRep).

We learned hand to hand combat, basically how to really hurt people with your hands if you ever lost your weapon or ran out of ammunition, I planned on doing neither if I was ever to deploy.

A week before graduation we had to qualify our weapons before we could be processed through graduation. If you failed, you would have been rolled to the next class to graduate with them, if you passed weapon quals then, I assumed that after so many failed attempts to qualify, you'd just be discharged.

Luckily for me, I passed the first time with 39 out of 40 targets hit. The highest qualifying rank is Expert, which is reached with hitting at least 36 of the 40, most people dubbed the 39-40 rank Hawkeye.

Since I was one of four Hawkeyes, and the first to do it in my platoon, I was no longer just Private, Maggot or Turd. I stepped up to High Speed Private, High Speed Maggot or High Speed Turd.

We were offered to spend the last week in jump school. After some strong persuasion and coercion from a few of my battle buddies, I agreed to go with them. Who turns down a few extra dollars on their paychecks right?

Me, that's who, and I should have. I made it through the first three jumps that were at low altitude. It was the fourth jump that got me, at 10,000 feet standing at the door for my turn to jump, I suddenly remembered how afraid of heights that I was. Bambi and I have got to be related, I started shaking harder than a stripper on a pole with an eviction notice and past due bills.

Once I told the jump instructor that I couldn't find any good reason to jump out of a perfectly functioning plane, he told me that it would be okay and I could return to my jump seat. As soon as I turned around he was smiling and he put his size 12.5 combat boot in my chest.

I was so in shock that he had just kicked me out of the plane that I didn't notice myself throwing up until it started hitting me in the face. If the parachute didn't have an emergency release mechanism that automatically pulled the chute when it hit a certain altitude, I probably would have woke up dead.

Needless to say, I didn't pass jump school and I didn't dare to volunteer for shit else. I graduated from basic training and that was good enough for me.

CHAPTER 7

Before I left the base, I had a little free time to myself so I decided to run to the PX and buy Tanner a nice ring set that came with the engagement ring and matching wedding band.

The night before, I had checked my accounts and noticed that they were untouched. I figured Tanner must have wanted me to propose in person before she started with the wedding planning.

She didn't know exactly when I would be home so I didn't tell her I checked my account, nor did I ask her if she caught the cold feet about getting married. I just told her I missed her and I loved her. I ended the call with an I'll see you soon.

CHAPTER 8

Before we landed I kept pulling the ring out of my pocket, wondering if I'd made a mistake. I figured it was obvious that Tan must have changed her mind.

Oh well, I've already purchased the ring, she was just going to have to tell me no to my face.

After I collected my luggage, I went to the pick up zone to look for my driver. I hired a limo service to take me back to the hood, G.I. Joe was about to pull up on the set in *style*.

When I spotted the driver holding the board with my name, I heard a loud shriek. I turned just in time to see Tanner launching herself at me.

What the hell, I thought to myself.

I caught her in mid air and hugged her for so long, it felt like time stood still and the world was watching.

What better time to get embarrassed in front of a bunch of

strangers than the one present. But first I had to get down to the bottom of something that was tugging at my nerves.

"What the hell are you doing here? You weren't supposed to know I was in town just yet."

"Why not, you had to go see another bitch first or something?" Tanner shot back.

"Now you know damn well that isn't the case. It was that stupid app wasn't it?"

"No, haven't you learned you can't get anything past me? I'm a college student, I've met all types of people from different walks of life. I had a friend teach me how to hack and shit. Everyday for the last two weeks I checked the airlines' manifesto, I knew exactly when you'd be arriving," she said with a smirk.

"You're such a sexy criminal. Why didn't you say anything when we talked yesterday?"

"The same reason you tried to sneak here, I wanted it to be a surprise."

"Well surprise, surprise. I've got a surprise of my own." I let her go and got down on one knee. "Tanner LeAnn, will you marry…"

Before I could finish she was pulling me up and burying her tongue in my mouth. I have never seen anyone cry a river and kiss at the same time.

When she finally stopped sobbing she pulled away and held out her hand. "Yes, oh my God. It's so beautiful!"

I slid the ring on her finger and the background came back to life and erupted with applause and cheers.

"Since you're here, I guess I won't need my ride anymore," I said after I wiped the tears from her cheeks.

"What ride?"

"That big boy right there," I said pointing to the Mercedes Sprinter van.

"Why in the world would you waste money on that? You too good for the bus or a cab now, Mr Soldier Man?"

"No, not at all. I knew you wouldn't be able to resist my pizazz if I pulled up and proposed to you after hopping out that joint."

"Just fucking stupid," she responded shaking her head.

"Now you sound just like my grandpa. Give me a second, let me go tell the driver I'll be riding home with you."

I apologized to the driver and explained what happened. He was understanding, seeing that he had already been paid anyway so I gave him an extra $100 tip for wasting his time.

He thanked me and gave me his personal number to reach him if I needed anything in the future.

Once we got in the car I jumped right into it. "So what's going on, why didn't you pay any deposits for the wedding? I wanted to have everything done and out the way so when I got here all I had to do was pick up my tux."

"Shut up, I don't want to talk about that right now. We have all night to discuss that."

"Oh, but we aren't doing anything sexual until we have this discussion."

"Yea I'm sure you'll change your mind. Don't worry, if I have to roofie you, I'm getting in them drawls," she said slyly.

"Wow, that just got dark. Where the hell are you going? You just missed the exit."

"Red Face, just sit back and ride please? I have a stop to make really quick."

CHAPTER 9

When we pulled up to Union Station, I was confused. "You couldn't have dropped me off and then came and visited your family in the aquarium?"

"Wow, you really just called me a sea creature?" she asked hurt.

"Yes, a beautiful mermaid, my love," I said as I leaned over and gave her a kiss.

"Get out and come on. Let's go get something to eat and we can discuss this wedding over dinner."

"Babe, we could have came and ate after I saw my family."

"Just come on, you talk too much." She took her phone out and started going live.

As we walked up to Landry's Steakhouse I noticed the lights were out. "I think they're closed, boo."

"Nope, we've got the place all to ourselves tonight."

Soon as we walked through the door the lights came on and everybody yelled, "Welcome home!"

I think I heard one or two dumb asses say surprise instead.

My blood got hot and I saw red in my eyes. It took a second to recognize that those were my folks. My gun was in my hand before I knew it. I had to catch myself before I pulled it up and aimed it at somebody.

They thought it was just hilarious. I wonder how funny it would have been if I would've accidentally blown one of their asses down?

Tanner turned to me. "It's our engagement party babe."

On cue everyone yelled, "Congratulations!"

She hugged me so tight that I accidentally farted, good thing that it was silent.

I kissed her and whispered in her ear, "I'm going to flush your goldfish for this."

She laughed. "Go enjoy your friends and family, love." She turned and walked off holding her ringed finger in the air.

After hugging everyone and thanking them we all sat down so we could order our food.

The first thing that I noticed was that the place mats were wedding invitations. My wedding invitations.

"Tan, what the hell is this? There's no way that we can prepare for a wedding in two weeks."

Pop stood up and cleared his throat. "Well son, everything has been taken care of. If you would have gone to college, I was going to give you twenty thousand dollars so you wouldn't have had to struggle to get settled in during your first year. When Tanner came and talked to us about additional wedding list invitations, I asked if it wouldn't be too much of a hassle, I'd like to pay for the ceremony. Consider it a late graduation gift. I'm still not happy that you enlisted in the service, but

I'm proud of you for following your heart. With that being said, congratulations son, cheers to a life of happiness. And remember, a man is only as happy as his wife," he added and held his glass up.

"Twenty thousand? Pop, where'd you get that kind of money?" I asked dumbfounded.

"A thank you would have been nice. As far as the money, that's a mystery that'll remain a mystery and will follow me to the grave."

I went and hugged my grandfather.

"Thanks Pop, I love you old man. I can only wish to be half as great as you."

"No son, don't be like me, you're going to be greater than me, I can see it in your eyes. Now let's eat, I gotta go see a cat about a fish,"

"Pop, you're seventy eight, there's no way you're still having your way with the ladies," I teased.

"As long as there's those blue pills around, I'm knockin' 'em down."

My mom looked disgusted. "Ew gross. Dad, we're about to eat."

"Shut up Chelle, how do you think you got here? A test tube?" His jab was followed by laughter from the whole congregation.

I just shook my head. "Man, let's just eat, this topic just went way left."

I said grace then we ate and drank. Stories were told by both of our families. They already knew each other since our parents grew up with each other so we didn't have any problems getting along.

With dinner done, everyone wished us good luck and spoke on how they couldn't wait to see us at the wedding. We hugged and said our goodbyes.

CHAPTER 10

Since it was still kind of early in the day, Tanner said she wanted to ride the new Ferris wheel they built outside of Union Station. It was one of those ferris wheels that are private and enclosed so that they could operate throughout the year. Alcohol was even offered before the ride and of course Tanner had to have her a drink.

Once the ride started, it was time for interrogation. I jumped right in. "You know, I was afraid you were going to be a runaway bride when I first checked the account and saw that you didn't spend any of the money in there. How did Pop come up with the money to cover the wedding? Did you know he had the funds for me already? It just seems a little too coincidental."

"Don't be so sure, we have to make it to the altar still. And no, I didn't know. The day you proposed over the phone, I went to them for help with the guest list. That's when he proposed to cover everything. I thought it would be a good idea, one less thing you have to stress over."

"I guess that would make sense, starting out our matrimonial journey in debt could only spell disaster. I don't think I could have asked for a better life partner to spend a lifetime with."

"Till death due us part, right?"

"Till death due us part. So seeing that we don't have to stop on Ashland to see anybody now, what do you have planned for us for the remainder of the day?"

"Don't worry I've got a few things in mind. First, let's talk about this honeymoon. I know you have to report to your next duty station by January fourth, so I'll allow you to take us somewhere after you complete your AIT training."

"How do you know all of this?"

"A good woman knows to listen to her man. The answers are always in the venting sessions, soon to be husband,"

"So I guess you think you know me, huh? Where would you like to go? I'll request some time off in March and we can go wherever you would like."

"I was thinking on the lines of Hawaii, how about Waikiki?" she suggested.

"Waikiki it is then my beautiful future wife."

"I love it when you give me what I want. You know what else I love?"

"And what would that be, Tan?"

"The way you look in uniform." She stood up and walked to the bench on the opposite side of the ride. She hiked up her skirt and slid her panties to the side and started to play with her clit. She pulled her coat off and lifted her shirt so that her perky 34C size breast fell out into the open and started massaging them and sucking on her nipples.

I was in complete disarray. Luckily the windows weren't transparent. I began to unbuckle my uniform belt, I was going crazy in the pants.

She slid her heel off and slid her foot into my crotch to stop me. "No, just sit there and watch. Right now I just want to soak up this view." She slid her toes from my crotch to my chest.

I grabbed her foot and started gently caressing her foot. I felt her legs start to tremble so I took her toes and began to suckle on them.

Tanner snatched her foot back. " Don't touch me." Then she went back to playing with her clit and sucking on her breast. She put her foot back on my crotch and started making circles with her toes on my erection.

Oh, Tanner was working me so well, she teased me so good that I could have exploded from a simple touch.

She looked me in the eyes with a seductive, devilish grin. "You want to fuck me don't you?"

"More than anything in the world right now. I'm close to erupting and I haven't even touched you yet," I whined.

"Too bad Zaddy, you're going to have to wait," she cooed.

"You sure know how to tease a nigga, it's been three months. I'm tryna get in that thang and go berserk. I'm loving what I see right now, I'm fighting to keep myself from drooling in this bitch! I can taste you from here, damn Tan, baby you're dripping."

She started shaking violently as she creamed on the seats of the Ferris wheel. She fixed her clothes and her shoes, then she stood up and walked across the ride to straddle my lap.

We clothes burned and tongue wrestled for the duration of the ride.

Real PG-13 ish.

CHAPTER 11

When the ride ended we walked back to the car, but Tanner wanted to take a tour through the aquarium. She knew that after that performance on the Ferris wheel, she could have asked me to go steal the president of the United States of America and bring him back to her and I would have complied. Whatever Baby wants, Baby gets.

Over the next three hours we went through the aquarium, walked a tightrope course that goes over the mall and walked through the room of mirrors.

We laughed, hugged, held hands, joked, and played with the stingrays and fish in the petting area of the aquarium. I legit did not want that moment to end.

"Babe, it's getting late, how about we get out of here. I know you want to get out of that uniform," Tanner alluded.

"Love, I'd wear this uniform day in and day out as long as it's going to make moments like this come frequently."

"I've got something else I want to do before we head into the hotel."

"Yea, I know, you're hungry too? Dinner was a little early," I said, realizing that my stomach was biting my back.

She smiled and said, "Yeah, I'm hungry."

I insisted on driving but she said she wanted me to relax and just go along for the ride.

When we pulled up at Pure Pleasure, I looked over at Tanner. "What are we doing at a porn shop?"

"I was talking to one of my Pretty Girl Clique girls from high school and she told me about this spot and their variety of toys. I wanted you to be here with me to help me with things you want to use on me."

That baffled the entire fuck out of me.

"Quit looking like that Red Face and come on. We're wasting time."

She walked me over to the men's section when we got inside the store and said, "Pick out some items, I'll be right back."

"Where the hell are you going? You're just going to bring me in here and leave me looking like a weirdo?"

"Boy shut up, I've got a surprise for you. Now pick some items and I'll be right back," she said again.

When she got back my arms were full of goodies.

She inspected everything. "Lube, wands, anal dildo, bed ties, door swing, what the hell is this? Virtual reality porn, no, everything else put on the counter. Put that virtual shit back!" she ordered.

"It ain't like I can touch them boo, it's all in my head."

"I said put it back, neow!" she said with her lip tight. "And hurry up before we miss the movie."

"Movie? What movie?"

"Just put the shit on the counter and follow me."

She led me further back into the store. We came to a hall that had six doors on each side of the hall, they looked like dressing rooms.

I was thinking she was about to try on some lingerie to model for me.

WRONG-O

I went in first, she closed the door and pressed play on the screen. A porno came to life, what did I expect, this is a porn store.

She started undressing me and used my uniform coat as a pallet along with her coat to cover the bench seat. She sat down and leaned back and started rubbing her clit again. Her last instructions on the Ferris wheel were "hands off" so I stood there and watched.

She took her foot and played with the bulge in my pants. Then she brought her toes up to my mouth. "Now you can touch me."

As I started sucking on her toes, she started gyrating her pelvis harder so that her finger could go deeper inside of he vagina.

Tanner climaxed and stood up putting her fingers into my mouth and feeding me her sweet sensation. She guided my hand to her throat and squeezed just enough for her comfort.

I wanted, no scratch that, I needed her so badly. I buried my tongue deep into her mouth. I could feel her breathing getting heavier as she came close to another climax. I had other plans though, I sat her on the bench and knelt before her.

Her clit touched my tongue and I started licking and sucking at the same time, her body began convulsing. She kept repeating, "I love you." As she got closer and closer to her euphoria she got louder and louder.

She came and I ate it all like the last scoop of ice cream in the middle of July.

Tanner pulled me to her so that she could taste herself. She unbuttoned my pants and pulled my rod out. "I know you want in, but it's been three months and I don't need you coming too quickly."

She pushed me against the wall and knelt down. Tanner looked me in the eyes and took my shaft into her mouth. First she started just sucking my head then she went deeper and deeper until I was inside of her throat.

I led her hands to the base of my joint and she immediately found her rhythm with the twist and pull. Ten minutes later I came and she didn't miss a stroke. She sucked me soft then back hard again.

Tanner pushed me onto the bench and straddled me, taking me inside of her slowly.

I looked her in the eyes and I saw the pleasure that she was feeling. "You're just full of surprises, aren't you?"

"This is only the tip of the iceberg," she moaned.

"So what other surprises do you have for me?" I asked intrigued.

"If I tell you, it wouldn't be much of a surprise, now would it?" she said smartly.

I bit my bottom lip and wrapped my hand around her neck. With that I guided her down harder until she squirted all over my lap.

She followed my gaze to the flick. "I want you to fuck me exactly how they do on screen. If they change positions, you change positions. Anything except anal, I'm not ready for that just yet. You think you can handle that, Zaddy?"

What sense did it make to answer that question when I could just show her. I picked her up and put her on the wall and gave her every inch that she wanted. Every position the movie did, I did. She wanted porn dick, I gave her porn dick.

By the time I came, she was shaking uncontrollably from cumming so much and her vagina was swollen.

"I desperately needed that Bae, the rose is good, but it's not the real thing. Get dressed and we can order some Imo's when we get back to the room."

We purchased the toys that I picked out in addition to a few that she picked out as well. The cashier kept trying to sell us on the public theater session, a larger room than the privates with other couples in there screwing. We promised to take a rain check then we headed to the room.

CHAPTER 12

When we got inside the hotel room I ordered the pizza from Imo's and we got in the shower. She cleaned me and I cleaned her.

Then we just sat there and held on to each other for dear life with the water raining over us.

We were still hugged up in the shower when the pizza man knocked on the door. I had to answer the door in my robe, still wet.

The tv watched us while we ate pizza until we couldn't be separated any longer. I lost count of how many orgasms we had. I fell asleep inside of her.

CHAPTER 13

Tanner woke me up to a kiss the next morning. She went and bought us breakfast from the cafe. When I sat up to take the platter from her, there was a note folded on the tray. $40 was taped to the inside and the note read: Your payment for an amazing night.

I looked at her crookedly. "Oh so now I'm your forty dollar hoe?"

"Nope, you're just my hoe. The forty was just a tip so don't get used to it," she said with a smirk followed by another kiss. "Now eat and shower, we have plenty to do today."

Dressed in my basic combat uniform, BDUs, I stepped out of the conjoining shower room. Tanner looked at me and shook her head. "Take it off."

I looked down. "I thought you love to see me in the uniform. Besides, what am I supposed to wear? All I have in my duffle are uniforms and work out clothes. Unless you want me to wear the outfit that I wore to basic training, I'm sure I can't fit that anymore, arms may be too big," I said flexing my muscles.

She pointed to the closet, which was full of clothes and they were in order of how I was supposed to wear them.

This woman is full of surprises I thought to myself. "When did you have time to shop for all these clothes and shoes? I wasn't sleep that long."

"The day you told me you were coming home for Christmas, I started buying things and putting them up. Yesterday before I came to the airport, I stocked up the closet here. I told you yesterday, that surprise was only the tip of the iceberg."

"I can only imagine what else you have up your sleeve," I said looking for her to throw out a hint.

She didn't fall for the bait. The first outfit she had picked out was a silver red and blue Born2Win jumpsuit with a pair of butter wheat Timberlands topped off with a red Anaheim Angels hat. The undershirt had our prom picture on it.

"Don't you think the picture shirt is a little over the top, babe?"

"We're doing wedding shit today, are you too embarrassed to wear my face on your shirt?"

"Forget I asked." I knew better than to get into that conversation, there was no winning it at all.

Our first stop was the tuxedo shop. All the groomsmen already had their measurements done so their outfits were already finished and ready for pickup. I had to do a final fitting. They took my measurements to match them against the ones that I sent from boot camp. Then they hemmed it up the way that I wanted it and told me that it would be ready to go in a week.

Next stop was the wedding ceremony location. Tanner rented out the Masonic Hall for the actual wedding, the reception would be held at the Omega Center.

The cake design was emasculate. It was a five tier cake sitting above a chocolate fountain.

She booked the caterer and the photographer. All I had to do was find a DJ.

My boy DJ Greezy was more than happy to spin at the event. He was wondering where his invitation was anyway.

Once we finished everything for the wedding, I worked up a major appetite. St. Louis is known for its Chinamen, Chinese food for the politically correct, so it was only right that I hit up the China House. They're a biracial couple, Black wife, Chinese husband and they fused soul food with Chinese food. One word, DELICIOUS.

I had to grab myself a St. Paul sandwich, an order of crab Rangoon

and a Happy box with chicken fried
rice, no onion. Heaven in every bite.

Next stop: ASHLAND AVENUE!

CHAPTER 14

Tanner went to her parents house after dropping me off at mine.

I gave out hugs and sat in the living room and ran through the events of basic training. I told them how much I loved being a part of something positive for once.

Everybody seemed happy, but what they wanted to talk about more was the wedding and wanted to know if I was ready to take that step.

After I finally persuaded them that I was confident in my decision, I texted the gang's group chat and let them know I was on the set. It was time to get outside.

We all posted up under the tree that all the old heads hung under when we were coming up. We talked our shit and play fought, just like the old days. It was good to be home.

Our hood is in the heart of all the bullshit, it didn't take long for the shots to be heard in the distance.

I clutched my own gun because you just never know.

Shoota started laughing. "Aye G.I. Joe, chill out dude, you ain't in Iraq yet. That's Gwalla and Eyes warming up the Lex."

"So that shit still ain't died down yet huh? The winter is normally peaceful around here plus this muhfucka just like Iraq shit," I said as I relaxed.

"Man since you left, shit been hot round this muhfucka. I had to leave school to come and make sure the lil' homies were straight."

"Y'all got that nigga Eyes pressing shit now, y'all wild for the broyo."

"Shid, he tryna live up to your name, gang, lil' bruh thinks he is the gunslinger of the Wild Wild West now," Shoota informed me.

"Shoota bruh, keep an eye on dude bro. I'm holding you accountable, gang."

"Nigga the only thing you need to worry about is that wedding, potno. We got this down here, we're still up, they ain't hit shit yet," he laughed.

Lazy and Sanchez co-signed, "Yea, we got this bomb ass stripper party set up for your bachelor party, gang."

Eyes and Gwalla came running through the gangway. Eyes was smiling.

"We just caught Lil' O lacking, put his dick in the dirt," he said as he dapped everybody up.

I couldn't do anything but laugh because I couldn't be a hypocrite, he was only doing what he heard about me doing. What little brother didn't want to be like their older brother.

I did give him a nice talk though. "Lil' bro, you gotta be careful when you slide on something, mask up, glove up and trash your outfit that you slid in. No evidence, and go in the crib and wash your hands with bleach right now. You know them niggas are going to point down this way first."

Him stepping with people that I trust made me feel better than him going with some unknowns.

One thing people could never say was that we back door each other. AAG niggas were loyal to a fault, death before dishonor.

My phone started ringing and I knew it was Tanner before I even looked at the caller id. "Where the hell you at? They said somebody got shot down on the Lex, you know Ashland is the first place they're going to come to."

"Babe chill, you know we blicked up out here. If they slide through they won't make it past the top end," I responded trying to ease her mind.

"I don't give a fuck about any of that, you got a wedding to make it to and a career to get back to. As a matter of fact, put me on speakerphone." When she knew it was on she went in, "If anything happens to him before my wedding day, I will personally kill each and everyone of y'all out there," she threatened.

Shoota wouldn't be Shoota if he didn't have a smart comeback. "Tanner ain't nobody scared of you except G.I. Joe. Ain't nothing going to happen to dude. We finna shake from down here anyway."

I took the phone off speaker. "Why do you always have to embarrass me in front of my friends, Tanner?"

"I can care less how your friends feel. My concern is your safety, I'll be around there in about three minutes. Be ready to get your ass in the car!"

We hung up and I dapped my boys up. "Make sure y'all send me the info for the bachelor party."

Sanchez said, "You know Tanner ain't going for that."

"We'll kidnap his ass if she say no, as a matter of fact, does the tux company have a delivery option? We're going to be too fucked up to try to pick up the tux that early in the morning," Lazy said always seeming to save the day.

"I don't know for sure, I'll have Tanner call and check. I'll let y'all know in the group chat. In the meantime, put the info for the party in there. I'll holla at y'all boys later, stay dangerous," I said as I started to walk back up the street.

In unison we all said "A's up or K's up till my days up!"

Over the next week and a half Tanner and I stayed close to the vest. She was not letting me out of her sight, she knew that it would be easy for me to relapse and be sliding on the Lex with the gang.

We did some sightseeing as if we were tourists. We searched the Explore St. Louis website which led us to Six Flags, Meramec Caverns and Amp Up Action Park. Anything to keep me from thinking about the hood. I can't say that I could complain, we had a really extravagant time. Plus unlimited sucking and fucking.

Party day, Tanner didn't put up too much of a fight because she was having a bachelorette party herself. She wanted to follow tradition and spend the night separately.

Before I jumped in the car with Fatt Rell, she hugged me and kissed me hard. Then she squeezed my dick painfully. "This better remain untouched tonight or you'll be dickless tomorrow. I dare you to try me."

"C'mon Baby Love, what do you think this is, Junior's bachelor party or something? Just make sure you don't have no dick in you or we're going to have some problems, I'm the first and last to tap that ass. Understand?" I stated firmly.

"Yes Zaddy," she cooed playfully.

Fatt Rell got started as soon as I sat in the seat. "I was about to be pissed, I thought y'all were about to to start fucking on my hood."

"I'm pretty sure I could have. When you're good to your bitch, she'll give you the world my boy," I answered.

He nodded in her direction as she was walking back inside her mom's house. "That one will take your world if you're not careful."

"That's what attracts me, gang, the shit is dangerous. I love that she'll pull up and play ball. She doesn't mind beating my ass on the block in front of y'all," I laughed.

"A'ight dawg, that's a little TMI. Let's go meet up with the gang and see some booty meats getting clapped."

Two knocks, that was all it took for the hotel room door to be opened. Standing there were two exotic women dressed in business suits. Before I could apologize for coming to the wrong door, they snatched me inside by my shirt.

The party came to life before my eyes, it was booties and titties everywhere. They had four shots of Patron lined up for me before I stepped past the welcome mat.

We were in the presidential suite at the Ameristar. There was a kitchen, living room, jacuzzi in the bedroom and a large window overlooking the outdoor pool. My boy really outdid themselves.

Within ten minutes my phone rang, and yes, it was none other than Tanner.

"Aren't you supposed to be getting ready for or enjoying your own bachelorette party?" I asked.

"I'm about to, but I want you to have FaceTime on so I can make sure you're behaving yourself."

"No, I'm not doing that. How are we supposed to be getting married tomorrow if you don't trust me?"

"I do trust you, it's hoes that I do not trust," she answered defensively.

"Tanner, they can't do anything to me that I don't allow and I'm not on any of that."

I hung up before she could protest and sat the phone on the dresser in the room. She could use her app if she wanted to check in.

It was some booty meats that was in desperate need of my slapping.

CHAPTER 15

After a long night of Patron shots, I had a hangover from hell. It was definitely worth it though, the strippers gave me a great show, they danced, stripped, gave lap dances and they did a bubble show for me in the jacuzzi.

They ended the night by giving me my personal freak show. Four of them had a mini orgy on the bed while I sat and watched from the jacuzzi. I wanted to join in extremely badly but I stood on my word and fought the temptation.

Thank God Lazy recommended getting the tuxedos delivered because I only had about three hours to sober up before the wedding. I needed every minute of those three hours to get my shit together.

When everybody woke up, we ran to the city to grab some grub. The best way to sober up is bread and grease, heavy grease. We hit up Billy Burke's, the best burger joint in the city.

Four greasy burgers in, my hangover was lifting and I was ready to get to it. We arrived at the Masonic Hall with an hour to spare. I had Lazy, my super secret best man, to go and make sure everything was in order with Tanner.

Our tuxes were in the groom's quarters so the rest of us went straight there to start getting ready.

I started to get nervous and I needed a shot badly. Sanchez was already ahead of the game. Out came the Hen-dog.

Lazy came back and told us that everything was good to go except the limo service couldn't get a driver for us and Tanner was tripping.

The Hennessy kicked in and helped calm my nerves so I remembered Big Chris, the driver from the airport.

I instantly dialed his personal number. "Hey Big Chris, how's it going brother? This is Keefer Khrist, the guy from the airport who's girl picked him up instead."

"Yeah, I remember you buddy, what's going on?" he asked.

"I know it's last minute, but our wedding is today and the limo service we hired canceled on us. I was wondering if you're free today?"

"I am free but the only vehicle I have available at the moment is a Mercedes S63. I don't think you'll be able to fit a wedding party in there," he said while he laughed.

"Don't worry, we'll take it. Thank you my friend, you're a lifesaver. We'll figure out the rest. I'll get the information over to you now."

Lazy went and relayed the message to Tanner that I found a service that would chaperone me and Tanner, but the rest of the party would have to get to the reception on their own.

It was her day, I didn't care about anyone else at that moment. Fortunately they agreed to make it

work as well so long as the bride
was happy.

***

The wedding bells were ringing,
organ keys were singing and my
stomach was getting more and more
uneasy.

I was in place at the altar when the
doors opened up and the wedding
party started to file down the aisle.
They were followed by the flower
girls who covered the aisle in red
and orange rose petals.

Finally, the organ player switched
to the formal "Here Comes The
Bride" tune.

When Tanner walked through the
doors I instantly started shedding
tears. That moment was the most
beautiful sight to see. I wanted to run
to her and run her back to the altar. I
needed to get her to the stage with
me stat!

She arrived at the stage and I met
her at the bottom step to receive her

from her father and walked her up the stairs arm in arm until we reached the altar. Removing her veil choked me up even more and my legs got a little weak as I thought, my woman is gorgeous. I couldn't believe I was actually going to be the one that married her.

She rubbed my hand and mouthed, "It's okay."

The ordained minister brought us together in holy matrimony, we said our "I do's" and our vowels.

"You may kiss your bride," he said to me.

I took a long look at her before I kissed her so that I could watch her beauty into my brain and cherish it for a lifetime. The first kiss sent chills up my spine. Marriage magnifies every sense toward your spouse, taste, touch, smell, sight and hearing.

As we walked outside to get in the car, the crowd showered us with rice. A rock or two may have been thrown as well, knowing my family and friends, I wouldn't be surprised.

On the way to the reception venue, our mouths were locked together the entire ride. I didn't even notice that we had pulled up until Big Chris opened the door for us.

CHAPTER 16

The reception was really elegant. Me and Tanner's plates consisted of porterhouse steaks, lobster tails, garlic mashed potatoes and a Ceasar salad. Our wedding party was fed sirloin steaks, shrimp, pasta and a garden salad.

The guest had the option of chicken or chicken, pasta or potatoes, breadsticks and a garden salad.

Lazy did the best man toast, which didn't sit well with the other homies.

Tanner's maid of honor did a toast as well. She finished it off by saying that she's glad that the process was over because she was up to her limit with Tanner being a bridezilla.

Pop's toast was his usual, short and sweet. "Remember, happy wife, happy life." A man of very few words.

Tanner sat in a chair so that I could remove her garder from her leg before we did the first dance. I decided to remove it with my mouth instead of my hand when I put my head under her dress. I licked up her inner thigh towards her vagina and she tensed up and pushed my head away because she knew that I would lick her pussy right there in front of everybody. She was my wife now and I made the rules.

The first dance, DJ Greezy played Differences by Genuwine. Once we finished our dance, Tanner and her dad had a dance.

After their dance, my boy Greezy knew to jump over the ratchet music. He played hood songs like Boosie and Webbie and the gang went crazy. The whole dance floor was all AAG and Tanner, we were all stacking and twisting our fingers up. Word for word, we set it off in that bitch.

When you heard, "This is for the nine nine and the two thousands," you knew it was about to get real. All the hoe-ness came out of the women. Soon as the beat dropped, the booty meats dropped. Even the studs were shaking ass. Juvie was undefeated.

Tanner told me to come here. She started twerking on me so I leaned back and let my guys hold me up. Old school, I know right?

The whole reception was just all around fun. Smiles and laughter everywhere. Only bad part about it was that it had to end eventually.

Greezy announced that the last song was about to be played. He took us out with Let's get married by Jagged Edge.

We took one last group photo then the party was over.

The wedding party was the last to leave the building after the guests were gone. You could tell that something was wrong, things were extremely quiet and eerie. We were in the ghetto, no matter the weather, it doesn't get quiet.

Wheels started screeching and the shots rang out. Two black Chargers were sending shots our way.

My first instinct was to push my wife to safety, but she had been through situations like that before, she was already ducking behind cover.

My next motion was bringing my gun up. Everyone was already returning fire, even Big Chris, the driver. Those black Chargers were receiving the twenty one gun salute.

Somebody hit one of the tires on the second Charger and it lost control then crashed into a light pole.

Shoota, Deuce, Reddot and I walked them down. One tried to run but Reddot put the brakes on buddy real fast, emptied the clip on him.

Shoota and Deuce took the two in the back seat and I put my toe on the driver. Try to ruin my day, I'll kill yours, dead.

Gwalla was on the ground bleeding when we got back to the

Omega Center's parking lot. He got hit in the arm and foot.

Big Money brought his Jeep SRT around so we could go after the other Charger. As soon as I opened the door to get in, Tanner grabbed my arm.

She had tears in her eyes. "Please, not today. It's already bad enough they shot up our wedding. I need you to sit this one out, I'm begging you, Red Face."

As much as I hated to admit it, I knew that she was right. I needed to stay there and protect my future, my wife. I gave my throw away to Eyes and sent them ahead without me.

Animal and Stuck drove Gwalla to the hospital, ignoring every red light.

Big Chris, Lazy, Fatt Rell and I started picking up the shell casing on the Omega Center's lot.

By the time the police and ambulance arrived on the scene, it looked like we were innocent bystanders caught in the crossfire. They questioned us and we told them that we didn't know anything, only thing that we knew was that shooting started.

We were told that we can't leave.

A white shirt pulled up and introduced herself as Captain Williams.

I shook her hand and in my opinion she held it a little too long for comfort and why was she giving me bedroom eyes while she was holding onto my hand?

"Do you mind if I talk to you over by my cruiser, Mr., I'm I didn't catch your name."

"Mr. Khrist would be fine, it's spelled with a k instead of a c, but it's pronounced the same," I informed her as we walked to her cruiser.

"You mind running me through what you saw?" Lt. Williams probed.

"I already told your officers everything that I saw," I answered tersely.

"I'd like to hear it from you because things can get lost in translation," she came back, keeping her cool.

I looked at her annoyed. "It's my wedding day and y'all are holding my wife and I back from enjoying this day. She's already shaken up because four people are dead in front of the first place we chose to have our memories as a wedded couple."

"I understand the frustration but you're the only person that saw something other than your friend that's laid up in the hospital right now. By the way, why didn't you mention that to any of my officers?"

"Because there's nothing to tell ma'am. Look captain all I saw was two black cars shooting at each other and saw the other one crash, then more shots rang out. My only concern was making sure my wife was safe. As far as my quote unquote friend, I wasn't aware of anyone being shot that was with us. Now if that's all, I'd like to get back to my family, I'm sure they need me more than you do."

"Just one more thing, you wouldn't happen to have a weapon on you would you?"

"Only weapon I have is my military issued sidearm, which I have my identification for. I'm not of age to own any personal weapons if that's ok with you ma'am," I said more as a statement than a question.

"I'll need you to turn that over to us so that we could run a ballistics test on it since it's in the vicinity of a shooting. I'll fill out all the necessary paperwork and send it up the proper channels."

"Good luck with that, because my weapon is at the Embassy Suites by the airport and I'm not aware of any shootings that occurred out there since I've been in town," I said as I raised my tuxedo jacket up to show her that I was unarmed.

She smiled. "Well aren't you just a clever one. Here's my card, if anything you remember comes up, give me a call." She winked and walked off.

After a long debate with Tanner, I finally had Big Chris to transport her back to the hotel. Lazy took me to the hospital.

Tanner called me as soon as she pulled off. "Baby, I want you to come to the room. Please don't do anything stupid," she begged.

"Boo, I got you I promise as soon as I make sure bro straight, I'm coming straight there," I committed.

"Ok babe, call me when you get downstairs."

Gwalla was laughing and joking like he didn't have two new holes in him.

Normally a gunshot patient would be on blackout but my grandma worked in the ER so she took us back.

Shoota FaceTimed me to check on Gwalla and to let us know that the other Charger was nowhere to be found around the Lex, it was a ghost town.

Animal and Stuck said they would stay on guard with Gwalla and they would let me know if anything changed.

As always we separated with the AAG credo, "A's up or Al's up till my days up!"

CHAPTER 17

Tanner met me in the hall, I texted her when Lazy dropped me off. She hugged me deep and buried her head in my chest when I walked up on her then she stood on her tip toes and kissed me.

"I have another surprise for you, but I want you to wear this blindfold so that it's not spoiled," she said, pulling a blindfold from under her robe.

Even though her 36-24-36 frame enticed the hell out of me, I still eyed her skeptically. "What kind of kinky shit you got going on babe?" I asked even though I still complied.

Tanner led me into the room blind, stripped me of my clothes and took me to the shower. She bathed me and I became so aroused that I was itching to feel the inside of her. Dried off, she led me into the living room and sat me in a chair, then I was handcuffed with my hands behind the chair.

"Mrs. Khrist, what the hell are you doing?" I asked because I was afraid of what was to come next. I had a really big fear of the unknown.

"Shhhh," she whispered into my ear.

I could feel her kneeling between my legs, then she started massaging my thighs and my scrotum.

Something felt odd but I couldn't quite put my finger on exactly what it was.

My dick entered her mouth. The way she sucked and stroked me was magnificent. I heard the vibrator, every man knows when a woman is pleasing herself while giving head, your soul is about to be stolen.

About three minutes later, I felt some wet shit hit my shoulder from the right and I jumped. "Damn Bae, you're squirting all over the place, shit hit the wall and bounced back."

I felt hands run down my chest and I started thinking, damn she's doing some acrobatic type shit.

Then she whispered in my ear again, "See what happens when you make your wife happy?" she pulled the blindfold off.

That was not my wife who had my cock in her mouth. My mouth fell open because I didn't understand what was going on nor was I about to stop it. The way that the woman rubbed my thighs and scrotum was what I felt was odd, I knew Tan's hands and the way they felt, I'm surprised that I couldn't tell by the head game that it wasn't Tanner. Don't get me wrong Tan's head was great but what I was experiencing at that moment was nothing short of phenomenal.

Tanner walked around me and sat on my lap facing her accomplice. She turned on her rose and put it on her clit. With the mystery woman sucking me still, Tanner said, "Eat it up friend."

So ghetto I said to myself trying to stifle a laugh.

Mr. Rose was putting in overtime, Tanner started quivering and gyrating on my lap. Her climax was reached and she squirted all over Friend's face while she was still devouring my member.

Friend finally took a breath and put my dick inside of Tanner's pussy. Every ten strokes, she would pull it out and suck the juices off of it then stick it back in.

I took in the room, there were sex toys littering the room both on the table and floor.

Tanner stood up and pulled me up too. When she took the cuffs off and sat down, I thought that was my cue to eat her pussy.

She said, "No, I want you to fuck her while she eats my pussy."

Baffle meter broken. "This some kind of test or something? I don't wanna do that."

She got up and grabbed me aggressively by my meat and

pushed me to my knees and inserted me into Friend.

Friend started throwing them big ol cheeks back while reaching back to rub her clit while I stroked her.

"Fuck it up friend, fuck it up friend," Tanner said playfully. Then she sat down so that Friend could eat her pussy. Tanner squirted all over the both of us and I loved every second of it.

Next Tanner wanted to run a train on shorty. She put on a strap-on and laid down. Friend mounted her and Tanner pulled an anal plug out of Friend's ass and made her suck it.

I scratched my head, where did that just come from. Was her ass that big that I didn't notice the plug a few minutes ago when I was beating her from behind.. Gosh.

Tanner spreaded Friend's cheeks and directed me into her cornhole.

We fucked the shit out of her friend and she took it all like she was used to taking it like a pornstar. Her moans were full of nothing but pure bliss.

Tanner looked over Friend's shoulder and said "I'm craving you, Zaddy."

She took off the strap and made Friend get on all fours then she got on all fours over the top of the friend.

I didn't need her help or guidance, I went straight to my wife. I gave her the fuck of her life.

A few minutes later she said she wanted me to alternate between fucking them like that.

I reached my limit. "I'm about to cum Mrs. Khrist," I yelled.

They both jumped up, friend knelt down, Tanner reached around me from behind and started stroking my dick until I came all over Friend's face while screaming the Mexican Grito.

I don't know who fell asleep first, but we had sex all night until nobody else was awake. If getting married comes with this, then marry me everyday of my life!

CHAPTER 18

I woke up unsure of myself. Last night I had the wildest dream, my wife and I had a threesome on our wedding night, I thought to myself.

I sat up in the bed and looked around and realized that I wasn't dreaming. Friend was cuddled up with Tanner. A smile spread across my face.

I went into the bathroom and closed the door so I wouldn't wake the women while I took a shower.

When the door opened I expected it to be Tanner, instead it was Friend.

Friend slid the glass door open and stepped into the shower with me. She whispered in my ear, "She wants you to slut me out while she watches."

The bathroom was connected to the bedroom so you could see the shower from the bed. Tanner was laid back on her elbows shaking her head yes.

Friend turned and faced the wall. I pushed her top half forward and gripped her dreads and slid up inside of her.

She gasped on the initial penetration but quickly regrouped and started pounding back on me. I put my free hand around her throat and went to work. I looked over at Tanner and she was giving me the show she gave me on the Ferris wheel.

Getting her hair pulled and choked at the same time did something to Friend, she went ballistic on the dick. Cream was everywhere on my pole and base, she started moaning more and more erratically. Her legs began trembling and she said her first words, "Why are you fucking me like this?"

Tanner walked in and started kissing me while I was fucking Friend. She ran her finger down my body until she met with Friend's cheeks and proceeded to finger her anally.

The pressure was doing its job. My stick started throbbing and Friend pushed Tanner's mouth to my dick so that she could suck the cum out of me. They French kissed as they came together.

We went to Tuscano's for lunch when we finished getting dressed after our shower.

It finally dawned on me that I didn't even know the girl's name. "So wifey, are you going to formally introduce me to Friend?"

"I'm sorry boo, I've been so caught up in the moment that I forgot. This is Day."

"Hi Day, it's nice to finally have a name for you," I said, kissing the top of her hand.

She replied, "It's finally nice to feel the hype that Tanner has built up about you. I can agree and I definitely appreciated every word."

I eyed Tanner. "Hype huh? So how did you ladies meet?"

Tanner took the query. "Soooo, I haven't been completely honest with you. And before you blow your shit, no I haven't had sex with any men. While you were in training, I started to get a little lonely. One night we had a little too much to drink and one thing led to another and we were eating each other out. It was almost daily afterwards."

"And you never mentioned this to me before, why?" I challenged.

"Because I didn't know how you would respond to it honestly. That was the reason for me introducing her to you last night, I figured that would be the best way to bring it to you."

"What man in their right mind would have a problem with their woman being bisexual?"

Day spoke up, "Oh you'd be surprised."

I shot her a look. "You sound like you speak from experience."

"Yes, but nothing like the last twenty four hours, this is the best that I've experienced. Most men aren't secure enough to introduce toys or another woman into their bedroom."

"She's the one that gave me the idea of taking you to the porn shop to observe your reaction. I saw how intrigued by the threesome scenes you were so we went ahead with our plan," said Tanner.

"So y'all just set me up huh? By the way, thank you Day, the porn shop experience is one to cherish for a lifetime."

We chatted some more until we finished our food then we headed back to the hotel so Day could get her car. Tanner and I went to the hospital. Big Money and Shoota were in the hallway talking in front of Gwalla's room.

I stepped in the room to talk to Gwalla first, who was in high spirits.

Tanner stayed in the room while I stepped back into the hall to holler at Shoota and Big Money.

"Any word on the streets about where that other car went?" I asked after we dapped up.

"Not really, the Lex has been real quiet. We've been riding through there periodically.

"Are we sure it was them?" I inquired.

Shoota looked at the TV over the nurses station. "It's been all over the news all morning, they showed all four of the ones we painted."

"Who were they?"

"The one that ran was Church, the driver was Big-O and the two in the back must have been some of their flunkies, I don't know who they were."

"Probably trying to catch a name for themselves. I know where Slew Kat stays, we can crush him tonight. I'll meet y'all in the hood around six after the sun goes down," I informed them.

Shoota shook his head. "Now G.I. Joe, if something happened to you, I'm not answering to Tanner. She's half woman half devil. And like every other time she's right, you got more than just the hood, gang. We'll be straight, I got us."

"C'mon Shoota, don't go soft on me, gang, I'm tied to this as much as the rest of y'all. Gwalla is in there with two holes in him because of my wedding."

"Nah gang, he's in there because he chose to go on a mission and they scored. That ain't on you, gang. That could have happened anywhere to any of us even if it wasn't at your wedding."

Even though I knew they were right and making perfect sense, I couldn't believe that everybody was being philosophers all of a sudden.

We left an hour later. In the car I side eyed Tanner. "You got the whole gang to go against my word. What did you do to my guys?"

"I didn't do anything, they just understand that it's more to life than that hood. I'm not saying to not love the hood, but eventually you'll have to move on from it. You're married

now, you have to think for your
family now."

CHAPTER 19

Two weeks later, it was time for me to depart for my next duty station.

I had to report to Fort Leonard Wood, which is only an hour and forty five minutes from St. Louis, so I left the night before I had to report.

Over the last two weeks Tanner kept me locked away in the hotel. We ate, fucked, ate, showered, fucked, slept and repeated up until we hit the road to Fort Leonard Wood.

Everything had been quiet in the hood so I didn't feel so bad about leaving them during the static.

Tanner on the other end was a different story, I had to pull myself away from her when she was dropping me off, I would have rather been with my wife.

She had to go to class the following day so I went on into the barracks.

CHAPTER 20

My primary job/MOS in the Army was 88M, a fancy way to say that I drive 18 wheeled trucks.

During AIT training we learned all of the transportation vehicles.

When we got to the tractor trailer portion of training I excelled because my mom and Fox drove over the road together for the previous 10 years of my life.

We were taught every type of driving that there is: offensive, defensive, evasive, tactical and how to set up security perimeters using your vehicles.

They taught us how to shoot at moving targets out of moving vehicles. We had to qualify for that as well. Yours truly finished at the top of the class, again.

We did night convoys or black out convoys in military jargon. Those are where the only lights visible on the vehicles are lights that are about an inch in diameter so that they can't be seen by insurgents from distances. Two in the front, two in the back.

We also did IED training. Spotters walked in front of the convoy surveying the road for imperfections that could house IEDs in the road. The insurgents are known for their improvised explosive devices.

After all the driving courses we learned some basic mechanic work for our vehicles. Those included tire changes, oil and lube changes and batteries.

The day before graduation one of the instructors pulled me aside. "Private Khrist, I'm First Sergeant Bechmeir, I was wondering if you'd accept an action to be deployed to our US Army Central Base in Kuwait?"

I was caught off guard. "I'm not sure I understand, my first two years are supposed to be non-deployable so that I can enroll into college."

"Yes, we've reviewed your contract and again this is an option, but if you accept then you could defer your G.I. Bill and kicker for up to ten years. You don't necessarily have to take it now."

"I'm very appreciative, but why me? Out of a hundred and fifteen soldiers that are about to graduate, why me?" I asked still confused.

"Well that's the thing, many of those soldiers need additional training. They either can drive or they're good at shooting, not too many of them can do both at this moment. You, on the other hand, can do both. You came in with some knowledge of logistics and weapons, a man went down in the theater and you'll be the perfect replacement for him."

"First Sergeant, I just got married in December and my wife is expecting me to take her on a honeymoon after I graduate. I think I would need to run it by her if that's okay with you?"

"Congratulations, how about I work some magic and get you an extra bonus to make the Mrs. happy, say, how about a nice fifty thou?" he asked with a wink.

"If you're married , I'm sure you understand that I'll still need to run it by her before I accept. She'll be here for graduation tomorrow and I'll ask her over dinner. If I get a nay or a yay, I'll let you know either way."

"Okay soldier, that works for me. I'll do what I can on my end. One more thing, soldier, remember a happy wife, happy life."

"Yea, so I've heard."

Tanner and I decided to grab lunch at Applebee's that was on base.

They say that you can't hide anything from a woman. "What's bothering you, Zaddy?"

"Nothing babe I'm fine," I lied.

"So we're lying to each other now? It's written all over your face and you've sat there and played with your straw for the last twenty minutes. What's going on?"

I sighed. "Yesterday one of my instructors pulled me aside and offered me the option to be deployed immediately."

"What about the non-deployable clause? Babe, we have a honeymoon to go on."

"That's what I told him and he said I could defer the clause for up to ten years, he also offered me a fifty thousand dollar bonus if I accept."

"Let me rephrase that, when do you leave again?" she asked with a laugh.

"So that's all it takes is a little cash huh?"

"Red Face, with fifty thousand plus your sign on bonus, we can go somewhere way better than Hawaii and still have some money left to put a down payment on a house."

"It sounds like you already have some type of plan. Also I'll have whatever I make while I'm over there, they pay us hazard pay while we're abroad."

"That's all the more reason to accept the offer and what do you think wives do all day? Sit around and just cook and clean? No, we have to think for our noodle brain husbands."

"You're putting words in my mouth, but what do wives do all day?" I asked jokingly.

"The things that husbands are too stupid to do, like finding a really nice house, decorate, budget, save and pick up y'all pieces."

"But are you sure that you're fine with this? I'll be deployed for a year."

"I knew the ups and downs of being a military wife the day I accepted your proposal. I didn't back out then so why would I now?"

"I just want to be clear so that there's no discrepancies in our marriage."

"Technology has made times like this a lot better, they have ways that we can video chat, that way we can see each other. Who knows, I may give you a show or two if I feel like you deserve it," she teased, sticking her tongue out and continued, "and if you're really lucky, I may give you a treat with Day when you're feeling down."

"Just when I'm feeling a little blue, that's it?"

"Maybe, maybe not. You'll just have to wait and see how it goes."

"I love you Tanner Leann Khrist."

"I love you too, tinky man."

"You just have to be gay don't you, like you just can't help it," I said with a frown.

"Nope, just bisexual. I thought you loved pet names."

"Well since you put it like that, I guess I'll accept it. And I do like pet names but some of them are too far."

"You'll get over it."

First Sergeant Bechmeir was excited to hear that I would be

accepting the offer. My orders were in my online file within an hour. I had a week to spare before I had to report to California for desert training.

CHAPTER 21

Back in St. Louis, Tanner was super excited about house searching so we started looking immediately for some that she liked. My opinion didn't matter, which didn't matter as long as she was in it and made it feel like home, that's all that I cared about.

I had to remind her that the bonus wouldn't hit until I reported to Cali because she was trying to move expeditiously.

She found a house that she liked in a nice suburban community called Barrington Downs.

The house had four bedrooms, three bathrooms, a living room, dining room, sitting room and a family room. The basement was finished with a theater room. The master bedroom had 2 large walk-in closets, a large bathroom connected that had his and her sinks, a jacuzzi bathtub and stand up shower. All complete with my favorite attachment, a 3 car garage and a roundabout driveway.

"Babe, don't you think this is a bit much for our first house? Especially seeing that it's only two of us?" I questioned.

"Husband, what's the purpose of buying something that we're going to grow out of?"

"Grow out of?" I hiked one of my eyebrows up. "You know something that I don't?"

"No babe, unless I can get pregnant through my throat, I doubt it. I just want to be prepared for the future," she said as she grabbed my member through my pants and continued, "because when you get back, you're putting babies in me. Like it or not."

"Is that right? What you goin' do, rape me if I don't?"

"If you don't hand it over freely then that's exactly what I'll be doing," she said with a shrug.

"And you're absolutely sure that this is the house that you want?"

"Yes big Zaddy, pretty please?" she begged while looking up at me with puppy eyes.

"When the money hits my account we can finalize the process and put the down payment down."

She jumped up and down. "Oh my God, are you serious? I thought we would have to wait until you came back."

"I want to come back to a home, not have to rush to find one. I can tell this would crush you if someone else got this house before I got back. Call the realtor, tell them that we'll be ready to give them the payment in two to four weeks tops."

Tanner hugged and kissed me. "I knew it was a reason I said yes to marrying you."

"And what was that?"

"Because you have no limit to ensuring that I'm happy."

"Oh that's all?" I asked playfully.

"That plus the fact that I can say, my man will come air this bitch out, at any moment and mean it plays a big part too."

I laughed hard. "I thought you didn't like it when I'm violent?"

"I don't like it when you do dumb hoodrat shit. The fact that you are violent makes my pussy throb."

"C'mon, let's get out of here before we tear these people's house up before we even put the down payment on it," I said as I started to walk toward the door.

Tanner grabbed my hand to stop me. "As a matter of fact, Husband, that's a great idea."

Uh oh.

We had sex in every room in the house. I don't know why but the room next to the master suite had the best vibes. We ended our last session on the kitchen island.

"You know what they say, blessing a new home like that is good luck for newly weds," Tanner said after we finished.

"Sounds like you just made that up."

"I actually did read that somewhere for real."

"Well regardless, with you as my wife, I have all the luck that I'm going to need," I said as I smack her on the ass on the way out the door.

She called the realtors and let them know that we liked the house and we would be contacting them soon with an offer.

We looked through some decor styles because Tanner wanted my opinion so that she wouldn't make it too girly. We agreed, we disagreed, but in the end she got the jist of what kind of furniture that I was into.

She even agreed to allow me to turn the theater room into my game room/ man cave. She knew how to butter me up.

For the next week Tanner allowed me to hang out with my family and the gang during day time only. She knew bad things mostly happened at night around our way.

We did everything from bowling, skating, arcades to bar hopping.

My last day, they threw me a going away BBQ in the hood. We blocked off the street and had a good old fashioned block party.

It lasted a good hour before the police came and shut us down by making us open up the street. By then everybody had come to me with hugs and well wishes anyway so we were okay with shutting it down. I was shocked that it even lasted that long since the hood was a war zone right now.

I hugged my mom, brother and sister and said my goodbyes.

Pop had tears in his eyes. "Remember to stay alert and keep your head down soldier." We hugged and said see you later because goodbyes are normally forever so we stayed away from them.

The gang all came to dap me up and tell me to keep my face up and stay dangerous.

"A's up or K's up till my days up!" You know we couldn't leave without saying the AAG farewell.

Tanner had Day meet us back at the room, they gave me the best farewell I could have asked for.

My flight departed at 6AM so Tanner took me to the airport at 5. We hugged and held onto each other and cried. I think I might have cried a little more. She didn't want me to leave and I didn't want to leave her.

With tears in her eyes she said, "Promise me you'll come back to me in one piece."

"I promise my love, nothing will stop me from fulfilling that promise either."

As I walked into the airport we held hands until the distance was too much. I kept looking back, I felt like I was leaving part of myself behind.

As much as she needed me, I needed Tanner ten times more, she was the glue to my world.

CHAPTER 22

I flew into LAX which is approximately 60 miles from Fort Irwin where I had to report.

First Sergeant Bechmeir reserved a rental for me so I could drive myself to the base and since I had a day and a half before I had to report, I did some sightseeing in LA.

I hit up Six Flags to see what the difference in their rides would be. The Goliath was my favorite of them all, when I pulled back into the ride station I asked the ride operators if I could go around again to collect my stomach from the last drop off.

Next stop was the Santa Monica Pier, I FaceTimed Tanner. We sat on the beach together and watched the sunset via video chat. It was the most electronically romantic moment ever.

My time was ticking so I needed to hit the road so I could get checked into the hotel before I reported in.

They offered me a room in the barracks but I would have enough of the barracks life over the next year, I needed some space and privacy. Before I left the city Tanner packed a Fleshlight in my duffel bag. We were going to have FaceTime sex up until my departure.

HQ checked me in and gave me instructions on where I needed to go for my training.

At 4AM I had to drag myself out of the sack, my body wasn't adjusted to the time change just yet.

Side note, whoever said time travel wasn't real is a liar, and a bold face one at that. I left St. Louis at 6AM and arrived at LAX at 7AM, I'm positive that I was on the plane for three hours. In your face non-believers.

Since I was on a special assignment, I was to be trained hands-on, one on one for the next month, they were adamant on getting me prepped to jump right into the hot zone.

The first day I had to pass a PT test. I passed the push-ups and sit-ups with flying colors, the two mile run however was a different story, I passed that with only three seconds to spare.

I don't know who came up with the two mile run idea, but in my opinion, it's STUPID. Who the hell is going to run two miles when they're getting shot at? Not I! I'm getting behind the closest obstacle and hunkering my ass down. But hey, maybe that's just me.

For the remainder of the first two weeks I had to participate in a bunch of classes that I had to force myself to stay awake. They consisted of: combat life saving skill, coordinate readings, how to spit IEDs, motor diagrams of the vehicles I would be operating, convoy procedures, tactical convoys, perimeter control, spotter responsibilities, turret systems for the vehicles, how to spot snipers and how to call in medical evacuations. Pretty much basic training on steroids.

I was called into HQ when I completed the courses.

First Sergeant Bechmeir held something back with our agreement, he put in a request to give me a promotion upon my completion of classroom training. The bonus he promised was also released into my account.

Thank you First Sergeant Bechmeir.

Tanner was excited to hear that the funds were in our account. She couldn't stop screaming through the phone.

"I'm so glad that I don't have to stay on campus anymore," she said after she stopped screaming.

"Why is that?"

"For one, I can come and go as I please and I don't have to be around these immature boys anymore. They act like pigs who have never seen a pretty girl before. It's smothering honestly."

"Since when have you not wanted male attention?"

"Since I married the most impeccable man in the world. The only attention of a male that I need is that of my husband. Besides, that day at the aquarium I was a tad bit jealous with all the attention you were getting from all those patriotic people that wanted to shake your hand for your service. I know how I felt and I would never want you to go through that."

"I'm hollering, but yet you sat and watched me fuck someone else and enjoyed it, how does that make any sense?"

"That was different, I was in control of those situations."

"If that makes you sleep better at night my lady," I said laughing.

"Whatever, so when can we move forward with the house, boo?"

"Actually you can call the realtor on three way now and get the process started. We can put in our offer for three hundred thirty since the bank approved us for four hundred ninety nine. That's fifteen thousand over the asking price. I'm sure we'll get it without a hassle. While I'm overseas you can get the house squared away without my distraction."

Tanner did most of the talking during the conference call, I didn't have a problem with that anyway being the financial backer was more of my speed anyhow.

By the time we got the paperwork finalized and the down payment sent over, the realtor company set up a closing date with Tanner.

"I had them to mail you another bank card to your mom's house so I can put some money in there for you to spend on luxuries while I'm across the pond. It should be there within a week."

"When did you go to the bank? And I can just spend the money out of the joint account that was frivolous," she stated.

"While you and the realty lady were jabbing y'all jaws. You need an allowance because you'll fuck around and spend the whole account, no lol."

"And here I was thinking that the male species was too incompetent to survive without female guidance. Imma let you get that lil' jab off since you just snapped with getting the house for me."

"You're a nincompoop," I joked.

"And you're a buffoon."

"Yo' mama is a baboon, the fuck."

"My point exactly. Idiot."

The next part of my training was all field training, which consisted of putting all the classroom work to the test.

They threw different types of traps and obstacles at me that I wasn't trained for. They wanted to see how

I would react and improvise on the fly.

Although it is highly unlikely that I'd be performing the duties, they took me through solo door kicking/breaching. I was a one man Army.

Each house that I breached had different traps. Some had visible traps and others had hidden traps.

The only trap I failed was the one that had a hole in the floor concealed by a floor mat. The ironic part is that the doormat had a smiley face and the words 'Watch Your Step' printed on it.

All the other traps I cleared easily.

The last house that I had to breach had a team of insurgents inside. As soon as I breached the door, they lit my ass up with paintballs.

The instructor stood over me laughing. "You're dead soldier," he said as he shot me in the face mask with a paintball.

Note to self: Never be the lead man on a breach team.

CHAPTER 23

The two week field training passed and HQ was satisfied with my progress. They said they were sure I would be able to survive down range safely as long as I had a team or a squad with me. They got a kick out of me getting blasted with paintballs.

Afterwards I had to take my physical exam and make sure I was up to date on my immunizations.

I was rewarded with two days of down time before I was to hit the skies to the Middle East.

Tanner insisted on flying up so that we could spend some quality time together before my departure.

While she was aboard her flight I drove to LA to book a hotel so that we could spend time in the city without having to travel an hour each way. And that was if traffic was constantly moving, which in LA was wishing upon a star.

We spent a lot of our time walking and shopping on Rodeo Drive. That told me that I'm going to have to put in overtime because Tanner could shop.

For dinner the homie Travis invited us to his crib in Beverly Hills. He said he was dining with some celebs and it would be dope if I dropped by and shared a meal with some locals.

Being that we were in Hollywood, I expected to see movie stars or musicians at the dinner. That was entirely not the case.

Travis grew up on Ashland with us and his mom invested in some stocks for him while he was in elementary school. By the time he graduated he was rich and decided to move out to LA, no one from the hood knew exactly what he was doing out there in Hollywood.

Dinner was full of pornstars. Travis was out there in the Hills living life like Hugh Hef. It was a big ass, literally, fuck fest.

The crazy part was that me and Tanner felt right at home so we joined the festivities, it was like we did porn professionally for a living.

Tanner said she was comfortable there so we canceled the hotel and stayed with Travis for my last free day. That free day was well spent.

Time flies when you're having fun but duty was calling and I had to answer. Tanner drove me back to the hotel by the base so that we could spend my final night cuddled up enjoying each other's presence.

Lift off was 0800 hours.

CHAPTER 24

Wheels down in Kuwait caught me by surprise, I slept the entire flight because I hadn't had any sleep before I left stateside. Not being able to be around my wife for a year had me in a somber mood.

Shortly after landing I found myself light headed. It took me about ten minutes to gather myself and my nerves.

When I finally stepped off of the C-17 Globemaster III, I instantly regretted it. It was hot as hell.

I assumed that since that was my first tour that I just wasn't used to it being so hot yet because the other soldiers didn't miss a beat.

I shot Tanner a text letting her know that I landed safely when I got settled into the barracks.

She called immediately. "Why didn't you call?"

"I wasn't sure if you would answer or not so I'd rather be safe than sorry."

"Smart man. So how long have you been there?"

"We landed about two hours ago. I reported to HQ and got settled in," I answered.

"What is it like over there? Does it look like home?"

"It's hot as hell, I mean unnecessarily hot. I haven't been off of the base yet so I haven't been able to see the country yet."

"So you slept from the airport all the way until y'all got inside the base?" she asked, not believing my answer.

"No babe, we flew into the base. We only land in secure bases in the military."

"So they let y'all use their military bases over there?"

"Baby this is the US military, we have military posts in numerous countries. Especially our allies," I informed her.

"Oh, okay I get it now, so we basically bully countries and demand a piece of their territory. That shit ain't no different from being in a gang."

"Sounds familiar doesn't it?"

"You were mine by choice, I didn't force you to do anything," she shot back, knowing exactly where I was going with my comment.

"Oh, so you grabbing me by the crotch in the middle of our high school hallway and telling me, this belongs to me now, isn't force?"

"You chose to say yes though so don't cry now," she said defensively.

"So what if I would've said no?"

"What's that? I don't understand that word. All I can tell you is I always get what I want.

"And I'll always give you what you want. Whatever you want," I repeated.

"I know. Is that the base that you'll be stationed at throughout your deployment?"

"No ma'am, normally we would stay here for roughly a month to get more training but I'm being fast tracked so that I can join the unit I'll be attached to."

"How long will you be in Kuwait? And where will you be stationed?"

"From my understanding I'll be here for two weeks then I'll be somewhere near a city called Al-Basrah in Iraq. What's with all the questions babe?"

"I'm just worried that's all, I know you'll be safe."

"It'll be okay, when I can call you, I will. I gotta run, Tan. It's time for chow and I have to get started with this training. I'll talk to you later, hun. Okay?"

"Red Face... I love you."

"I love you too, beautiful."

My assignment was to operate the turret on the commander's Humvee. I was excited about that because I was under the impression that I would only be a driver for my adoptive unit. Shooting was my passion, I knew instantly that I was going to love the position.

Over the next two weeks, I was brought up to speed with the layout of the land, threats, safe zones, hot zones and the rules of engagement.

They drilled the biggest rule of the Geneva Convention into my skull daily: DO NOT HARM a person that is unarmed or surrendering.

I had to stop the teacher. "So, Sgt. what if an insurgent shoots one of my battles then throws his weapon down, is he still eligible to eat a round of brass?"

"Unfortunately no soldier. Once he disarms himself, he is no longer a threat and can be detained."

"What would happen if someone were to eliminate him still?"

"You would be charged with a war crime. While in the theater, the best thing to do is pretend that someone is watching you at all times. That way you will always do the right thing."

"Basically practice integrity at all times, roger that, Sgt."

My ride pulled into the base to pick me up convoy style. The commander introduced himself. "Specialist Khrist, I'm Captain Millman. You'll be attached to my unit during your stay. We're a quick response team so we stay in the field to be able to give quick aid if and when needed."

"Sounds good, so what forward operating base is located in a hot zone?"

"FOB," he chuckled and continued, "soldier we won't be staying in the comfort of a fob. We're dwelling in a compound that was confiscated from an insurgent. You can tell that this is your first go round."

"What happens if said insurgent comes to reclaim their shit?"

"First, said insurgent is dead. Secondly, if that weren't the case and they came back to claim their property then we would protect it as if it were our own. Besides, we don't stay in one place too long. Every so often, we uproot and move on to the next location, that way it's hard for them to pinpoint our exact location."

"Sounds like a hell of a thrill, thank you for the opportunity to come aboard Capt.," I said with a salute.

"Great, let's get a move on. We have a four hour trek ahead of us and you don't want to be caught on some of these passageways when night falls."

"HOOAH!"

"Mount up, let's rock and roll."

Nightfall hit about thirty minutes after we arrived at the compound. Fifteen mansions covered the grounds inside the walls.

We stayed in the main mansion which was the largest house that I'd ever seen. Thirty bedrooms were inside the main house, each room had its own bathroom. There were three kitchens, an entertainment room that had a pool table, dart board game systems and arcade games. Whoever lived here previously was living like a king. The wall that surrounded the compound was a twenty foot wall.

We were fortunate to have eighteen military police attached to us so they kept guard of the compound 24-7. Everybody had a job to do. I would have been pissed if I had to pull night guard duty.

Captain Millman was precise with time, as soon as darkness hit the guns and bombs exploded in the night's distance.

It's like the insurgents were zombies or vampires and the light did harm to their ability to be bad people.

After dinner we were excused to our rooms. Each room was equipped with its own computer to video call your family since the cell towers didn't work for American phones in that part of the country. That's one amenity that I would be putting to good use during my staycation.

I sent Tanner an email for the chat link. By the time I got out of the shower she had everything downloaded and set up. And already calling.

"Husband! How are you?" said asked in a singing tone.

"I'm good, sexy face, just got to the new duty station a few hours ago."

"What's the name of the base so I can look it up and see where you're at."

"That's the thing, it's not a base, it's someone's house." I filled her in on the whole confiscation spiel and told her about my duties.

She was appalled. "Wow, that's deep. Be careful babe and keep your head down like your grandfather said."

"I'm actually going against that whole statement, the gunner position is on top of the vehicles. I'm going to be damn near fully exposed."

"I thought you meant gunner as in the first in the convoy. Why the hell would you have to be the sitting duck? What happened to driving, I thought that was your job?" she said, obviously frustrated.

"Welcome to the military babe, I'm the low man on the totem pole so I get the real shitty jobs," I lied. I was not about to tell her that I was excited about the position.

"Now I see why your granddad was against you enlisting."

"I know, but as a man I have to make my own decisions. Especially being married, how can I lead my family if I'm following someone else's lead?"

"I guess in that sense I can understand where you're coming from, but I still don't like it. I think it's stupid."

A loud buzzing sound filled the room then a voice came over an intercom. "QRF is needed at coordinates…"

"Babe, I gotta run. Love you, when I get back I'll email you pics of the mansion and compound," I said right before I blew her a kiss.

"I love you too, Husband, be safe."

Being that this my first time on a call I was gearing up on the move. I wasn't sure how much time I had to get to the Humvee so I made sure to be fast on my feet.

Before I got too far from my room I did a quick gear inspection:

Kevlar helmet, check.

Kevlar vest, check.

Kevlar arm and knee pads, check.

Uniform, check.

Combat boots, check.

9mm Ruger, check.

Ammo mags, check.

Rucksack, check.

Picture of wife, big CHECK.

M4 assault rifle, check.

iPod on Lil Boosie - Set It Off & Webbie - G - Shit on repeat, check.

It's stepping time.

My Humvee was the lead vehicle of the convoy, which in my opinion isn't smart because the commander shouldn't be the first to battle. But hey, I'm a newbie here, maybe that's just how this unit operates.

It only took us ten minutes to reach the convoy that was under attack. It was total chaos.

Three trucks were on fire and I could see at least four wounded soldiers.

Then shit got worse. There was a sniper's nest that nobody could locate. Over the headset they could only tell us the general direction where the shots were coming from.

While we had our thumbs up our asses the sky lit up. A mortar round was heading right towards us.

Our driver, Sgt. King did a last minute evasive maneuver and the round hit fifteen yards to the right of our vehicle. Dirt rained one me from the powerful blast. Thank God he paid attention in driving classes.

If you thought for one minute that that was the worst of it, you would be wrong.

I caught a glimpse of a flash up ahead.

"Top, I see the sniper's loca..." I wasn't able to finish my sentence.

I saw the round right before it smacked the glass of the turret, I dove down into the Humvee as fast as I could.

Captain Millman turned around. "Khrist, are you hit? You okay?"

I was in complete shock, I started feeling my body and was satisfied that I didn't have any extra holes that I wasn't born with.

"No sir, I'm intact. I saw the sniper's location, Top, permission to engage?"

"Roger that soldier, get up there and lay down some heat."

I jumped back into the turret and laid round after round into the window that the shot came from.

Unfortunately, the sniper had already moved from that position and was at a higher window.

I saw the shot just in time, I only ducked a few inches but it was enough to make him miss. The round grazed my helmet but the velocity of it was enough to knock the helmet off.

At that moment, Sir Lil Boosie of the Baton Rouge spoke to me from the hood trenches, "Set it off in this muthafucka, set it off, my clique all dogs, bitch don't make us set it off."

Time slowed down like some Max Payne type of shit.

I aimed my .50 caliber at the window that I saw the shot come from and unleashed a lead storm. I didn't stop until Captain Millman came over the headset.

"That's enough heat Khrist, bogey is KIA. Save some rounds for the next one."

"Roger that, Top, has anybody laid eyes on the mortar fire?" I asked, looking for more action.

"Already KIA soldier, stay focused and stay alert. We'll set up a perimeter to secure the hot zone until backup arrives."

"Copy that Capt."

We were anchored down for five hours until a convoy made it to carry the wounded and cargo back to the FOB.

Once they were headed back to the base our squad had to police the area. Any and all weapons and ammunition had to be retrieved, didn't want that to fall into the wrong hands.

Captain Millman put someone else on the turret and asked me to come help clean the scene.

Inside an abandoned building there was a wounded insurgent. After we breached the door he took a couple shots at us.

Sgt. King had a clear line of fire but Captain Millman yelled out, "Let the kid pop him."

I was the kid.

Capt' was in for a treat, haha, that was far from my first time with a close range kill. Two shots center mass, two to the dome, night night sucka.

By the time we finished securing the area, the sun was starting to rear its head. We had a stockpile of weapons and confirmed 18 kills.

Millman pulled out a pair of pliers when we finally got into the sniper's nest, he pulled out one of the sniper's teeth and tossed it to me.

"That's your first trophy, no matter how many you get, keep that one for good luck,"

"But I didn't claim one from the guy in the building back there."

"Doesn't really matter, the first kill is the one that's most important," Captain Millman said as he clapped me on the back while we were walking out of the door.

"HOOAH!" I responded.

Our last task was to set explosive charges on the weapon cache and our disabled vehicles.

As we drove away the explosive ordinance team sent everything up in a big fire ball.

Captain Millman released the unit from formation when we returned to the compound.

Before I could head in Captain Millman called out, "Specialist Khrist, I'd like to have a word with you in my quarters."

What the fuck did he just say, I thought to myself. "No thank you Captain, I'm not with any funny business. Women only for me," I said aloud.

"Me as well soldier," he shot back.

The whole unit erupted into laughter but I didn't catch the joke.

He looked at me and knew that I was going to stand my ground on them at one. "That's a direct order soldier."

I dropped my gear outside of the Captain's door, everything except my KA-BAR knife, I kept that in my pocket with my phone on record. Just in case.

"Close the door behind you, Khrist," Captain Millman instructed.

"Sir, I would rather not."

"Fine, suit yourself. I called you here to give you your first mission evaluation. I want to say that you did a great damn job out there, I expected you to freeze under pressure but you pulled yourself together and handled business like a true grunt. I think you'll fit in just fine in that position."

"Thank you sir, but we could have had this conversation anywhere but your bedroom," I stated, still uneasy about his choice of venue.

"I evaluate all of my soldiers in private. That way no one knows the next soldier's weaknesses."

"Am I the first to think something funny was going on?"

"This is a Don't-Ask-Don't-Tell Army now, but no you're not. If you would have responded any other way I may have been worried."

"Can I ask you something, Top?" He nodded and I pressed on, "Why did you tell Sgt. King to let me eliminate the target in that abandoned building?"

"All of my soldiers have had previous experience in wartime before they were attached to my unit. You are the first to be under my command straight out of boot camp. I know you can kill from afar but up close and personal is a whole different ball game. I know that you qualified as an Expert but I needed you to have your first taste so that I can count on you when the times get dicey. It was a part of your evaluation."

"Top, if I can be frank with you, that wasn't my first close range kill. I joined the service because I enjoyed doing these types of things growing up in the slums, I'll always be there when it counts," I assured him.

"Whoa. I don't want to know about anything that you've done illegally. Just remember, this isn't the streets soldier, you can find yourself in some real trouble if you unjustifiably terminate someone over here," Captain Millman warned.

"Copy, I just wanted you to know, when the time comes that I'll be in the game. You can lean on that!"

"After today, there's no doubt in my mind. Good job out there today, you're dismissed, soldier."

When I was back in the hallway Captain Millman yelled out, "You can let the knife go now, Khrist."

I looked down, I had forgotten that I had it in my grasp. Damn, was I tired. I ran through the house and snapped a couple of pictures of the mansion to send to Tanner before I hit the sack.

I emailed the pictures to her and jumped in the bed fully dressed in my combat uniform.

Sleep took me into its arms.

CHAPTER 25

At least I thought sleep took me into its arms, ten minutes after I fell asleep the buzzer sounded.

"QRF assistance needed at coordinates…"

FUCK ME RUNNING!

I'm glad that I hadn't taken my clothes off, I had to gear up on the run.

Somehow I was the last to make it to the Humvees and some dickwad wanted to test me. "What's the matter Khrist, your romantic morning lasted too long?"

"Nah bitch, I had a hard time getting off because I couldn't hide yo mama ugly ass face in the daylight."

Captain Millman stepped in between us and said, "Alright ladies, that's enough bickering. We have friendlies out there in need of assistance, let's mount up and go lay heat to some meat."

The unit sounded off "HOOAH!"

I was having an extremely hard time staying awake on the way to the mission. "Hey Top, any tips on staying conscious up here?" I asked through the headset.

He laughed. "Five Hour Energy drinks and Red Bulls, mix them together and you have yourself some crank in a can. Don't drink too much though, you'll burst your heart. You're a buck so you'll probably be able to handle more than the rest of us."

He passed me a 5 Hour Energy Drink to get me going.

That shit made me feel like a crackhead instantly. I couldn't stay still and it made me really jittery. That was going to take some getting used to.

Mission two wasn't as bad as mission one. When we arrived the area was already secure mostly and there weren't any casualties.

A Humvee had hit an IED and rolled over into an embankment. We just had to set up a security perimeter so that the unit that needed assistance could pull the Humvee out and flip it back over using a HEMTT wrecker.

Thank you Jesus it only took them forty-five minutes to get the Humvee upright and operational enough to make it back to the FOB.

Sleep was desperately needed in my life, I felt like I was about to keel over.

A pickup truck with a gun turret attached came into view when we got within five miles of the compound.

"Top, I have bogies at twelve o'clock with a turret mounted in the bed," I said quickly, hoping that he would understand.

"Hold your fire until you verify that they are a threat," Captain Millman responded.

The passenger raised his window down and leaned out of the window with an AK-47 and the turret gunner was bringing the barrel up towards us.

That was all I needed to see. I did not have time for that shit, I had a date with a king sized plush mattress and them cock suckers were not about to make me late for my appointment.

Fingers don't fail me now.

The first to eat lead was Turret Man, Mr. AK-47 got a mark of Buddha right on the forehead and his head exploded. I was in the zone and couldn't be stopped. The driver tried to speed past us so that I couldn't get a shot on him.

Oh no, don't run now.

His windshield turned crimson red after I pumped lead into his chest.

That's for trying to make me tardy for my slumber party.

As soon as I hit the bed I was out of it.

CHAPTER 26

Buzzz... "QRF needed at coordinates..."

I jumped up and looked at my watch, only three hours had passed by. Miraculously I felt well rested.

I wasn't last to the Humvees either.

We reached the coordinates but there wasn't anything going on.

"Uh Top, is this a drill or something? I don't see any friendlies or bogies," I stated over the headset.

"Just hang tight soldier, our target will be here shortly," he answered.

Shoulder shrug.

Twelve minutes later a convoy of American Military Vehicles were heading towards our position.

"Top, I'm not sure I understand, what's my objective here?" I asked out of confusion.

"This is a special convoy that runs from Al-Basra to Herat over in Afghanistan and back. We escort them to the next QRF and that is the end of our mission. Keep your eyes peeled up there. Let me know if you see any bogies, just like any other mission."

"HOOAH!" I responded.

Soldier Dickwad came over the headset, "Khrist if you're a good boy, Captain Millman might take you on another romantic evening."

"You keep trying me and you'll have a romantic evening with the morgue," I threatened back.

"What's the matter, you're that homophobic that you can't take a joke?"

"Some things you just don't play about, I ain't with that fuck shit."

Captain Millman came on. "Alright that's enough, everyone look alive, it's game time."

Top got out to greet the NCO in charge of the special convoy before we got in motion.

"Hey what's up Dirty. We got us a newbie in the ranks. So far he's been up to par so we won't have any problems," Millman said, shaking the newcomer's hand.

"So I've heard." Dirty looked up at my position on the Humvee. "Specialist Hawkeye in the flesh, nice to meet you."

"Same to you, Sgt?"

"Ghost but my friends and colleagues call me Dirty."

"I'll keep that in mind."

Dirty handed Millman a package and they went their separate ways. When Top got back in the Humvee he instructed everybody to switch to tactical frequencies on our radios. We fell into formation with the special unit, three of our Humvees up front and three bringing up the rear.

The first hour things went pretty good, then I spotted two insurgents covering up an IED on our current path.

"Top, I got two bogies at eleven o'clock covering explosives and at nine forty-five I got a couple mortars. Permission to engage,sir?"

"Negative soldier, stand down," Millman answered back.

The convoy came to a halt but I kept my .50 cal trained on the mortar boys just in case.

Three minutes later bombs obliterated the mortar boys. A spray of bullets were sent in the vicinity of the IED, it exploded when a round struck home.

"Convoy is commencing," Dirty said over the airwaves. "Good eyes up there Hawkey, keep up the good work."

"Anybody mind filling me in on what the hell just happened?" I asked, baffled knowing that I was showing my newbie colors.

"An AC-130 gunship trails the convoy in case of an emergency. We're the eyes of the operation and only attack in case of immediate danger. Keep doing what you're doing, call in any threats and we'll call it up and have the eyes in the sky wipe their noses," Captain Millman informed me.

"Roger that, Top."

Luckily that was our only encounter for that mission.

Back at the compound we voted on doing a BBQ for dinner. Since St. Louis is known for our BBQ so they begged me to be the grill master 3000.

Out of 30 QRF soldiers only seven of us were black and you could tell which dishes that we cooked because the ones that we hadn't cooked tasted like pure cardboard, flavorless. But hey, it beats eating them damn MREs.

My email notifications were blinking when I returned to my room, of course it was Tanner.

She called before I could read the emails.

"Hello beautiful, I was just checking your emails," I said answering the phone.

"I know, the video app shows when you're online," she told me.

"You're just finding all types of ways to spy on me huh?" I teased.

"Don't blame me, blame technology."

"Whatever, did you see the pictures of the compound?"

"Jesus, did I? Can we move there instead of the house in Barrington?"

"I thought you loved that house?"

"I did until I saw the mansion that y'all are staying in. It's absolutely stunning and I'm sure the pictures don't give it justice. I can only imagine what it looks like in person," Tanner said ecstatically.

I snickered. "Believe me, you wouldn't want to live in a war zone like this, hun."

"Growing up around y'all, I don't think it'll be too much of a difference, really."

That was the head scratcher of the day because there was nothing but truth in her statement.

"Well you have a point there. This shit is wild here though babe, I've been here two days and have already been on three calls. I like it but it wears on you, I'm exhausted"

"I wish I was there to tuck you in and hold you so you could get some rest."

"Would you breast feed me too?"

"Yes, you could fall asleep with my titty in your mouth," she answered, enticing me.

"Okay, I'm going to hold you to that. By the way, the closing is coming up, are you ready for that big of a step?"

"Zaddy, I wish it was tomorrow. I couldn't be anymore ready. I've been talking to Day and I think it would be a good idea if she stayed with me until you got back. How would you feel about that?"

"Why just until I get back, that would be rude to have her uproot herself from the campus and push her back out when I come home. I'm not that mean," I stated.

"I figured you'd want the house to ourselves when you got home."

"Baby, we have more than enough house for just the two of us, you have my full support on whatever you want to do. I like that idea more than you know."

"You just want to watch us have sex, you pervert," Tanner said, biting her lip.

"You know me oh so well my darling," I responded in a British accent.

"Oh yea before I forget, Shoota told me to tell you that Gwalla's mom made him move to Atlanta with Banga."

"At least that'll keep him out of the way for a while, tell them I said stay dangerous out there."

"I will and they sent their well wishes and said they miss you. Everyday they ask have I talked to you. They worry more than I do," she said with a sigh.

"Them are my guys, babe. Tell them if the Lex couldn't take me out then they know damn well some rag heads ain't going to be the ones to do it," I promised.

"Don't be so cocky baby, that's when people start to make mistakes, and every oops count. Especially over there."

"See that's why I needed you as my wife, you keep me grounded. I gotta get some rest while I can though babe. Never know when the alarm will sound."

"Okay, I love you, Red Face. Stay safe Zaddy."

"I love you more Mrs. Khrist. I'll dream about you."

We blew each other kisses and hung up.

Sleep took me as soon as I got out of the shower.

CHAPTER 27

The next four months were the same routine: eat, mission, sleep, mission, repeat. We did have a day or two here and there where we weren't called out.

Those days I used to catch up on some sleep and have some good old fashioned video sex with my wife.

For the days that she couldn't talk to me, she requested that I make some videos of myself cumming and moaning her name.

And I did it too, happy wife, happy life, right?

However, you can't please women. "Next time put the camera on the floor and let it splatter on the camera," Tanner demanded.

"Lady, you're crazy. I'm not about to do that, I record the videos on my phone and upload them. My face has to be on the camera when I talk."

"You don't complain when it's on my face, do you?"

"Now that's the sexiest thing in the world. But that's different, men shouldn't have their own bodily fluids anywhere near their own heads. That's extremely weird, you see how I tweak out when you let it touch my stomach now imagine it touching my face. No," I refused.

Tanner pouted. "But I want to watch the waterfall like I do in person," she whined.

An hour later I was scrubbing my phone with a Brillo pad.

During my fourth month with the QRF we were called out to a fire fight. When we arrived shit was already in the fan, total chaos. There were numerous casualties, multiple vehicles disabled and the bullets were still flying. The insurgents were firing upon the pinned down unit.

I thought to myself, why did our Humvee have to be the forefront sentry? No time to be timid.

My .50 cal was locked, cocked and ready to rock. I started sending rounds in every direction that I could see enemy fire coming from.

Two of our Humvees had gotten disabled in previous fire fights so we had them replaced with two gun trucks. Said trucks were equipped with two turrets and a separate turret for rockets, all joystick operated.

We were a force to be reckoned with and we secured the hot zone within twenty minutes of entering the theater.

Top was inside the perimeter helping with some of the wounded soldiers.

"Capt' I have a family of four enroute to our position, orders sir?" I called over the headset.

"Keep an eye on them, if they come closer than a hundred yards fire a warning shot. If they don't stop, light 'em up."

"Copy that," I said firmly. However, my nerves were fried, I'd heard about suicide bombers but that was my first encounter with them.

I sent a warning shot across the street from the family when they got within a hundred yard range.

Thank God they stopped.

No wait, they're moving again.

"Top, the parents are running away but the kids are still on course to us," I informed him.

"Do you see any bulges in their clothing?" Captain Millman asked.

"Negative Captain," I lied.

"Stay cold until they pose a threat."

Sgt. King came over the mic. "Khrist, take the shot! They're wired to blow! Engage, engage, engage!" he yelled.

Where I'm from kids and women are off limits so I couldn't bring myself to take the shot, even though they were running towards us.

"Dammit, take the fucking shot!" King screamed.

Next thing I saw was one of the kids top half of his body fall but the legs ran another six steps before they fell. The other kid took a round to the eye.

I looked down and Sgt. King was returning his Squad Assault Weapon to the rest position.

If looks could kill I would be dead.

Top came back over the headset. "Khrist, are you awake up there?"

"Yes sir, I'm awake."

In the distance I spotted the two parents running back towards their deceased children.

Warning shot.

They continued to run towards us. As soon as they took a step past the kids I ate their asses up. I seriously needed that day to be over with.

Within an hour we were relieved of our duty and heading back to the compound.

Top dismissed us and I started heading into the house.

Sgt. King stepped into my path. "What the fuck was that back there?"

I walked around him and went through the door.

He caught me in the foyer and grabbed my arm. "Look if you want to play with your life, do it on your own time. When I tell you to pull the fucking trigger, you pull the fucking trigger!" he screamed, spraying spit on me.

I wiped my face and looked at my arm that he had a hold of and said calmly, "If you don't unhand me, I will skin you alive."

He grabbed me by the collar.

Big mistake, my left palm hit his nose and it instantly bloodied. My right forearm crushed his windpipe after I drove him into the wall with it.

"If you ever even think about touching me again I would advise you to think ten times because if you decide to do it again, I will eat your fucking face."

He said hoarsely, "Go back to where you came from, the military isn't for your kind of people."

I released the pressure on this throat so that I could understand him clearly because he'd officially reached strike numero two.

"And exactly where should that be?" I asked.

"In a cotton field," he spat out.

Strike three.

My fist paired with his temple and his legs buckled. He was asleep before he touched the floor.

"And that's for DJango."

I went to my room and got in the bed, I was over that day.

At least I thought I was.

I was awakened by a knock on my door. Top opened the door without my consent.

"Khrist, did you assault Sgt. King?" he asked.

"No sir, I had been in the cotton fields all day, I don't know what happened in the big house," I answered like a slave.

"This isn't the time for games soldier, did you or did you not strike a NCO?"

"Nope, the walls must have hands or something, did you ask them?"

"Since you want to go that route, meet me at the Humvees in fifteen!"

Five hours later we were pulling into Camp Arifjan, the Army Central Base in Kuwait.

Sgt. King still had all of his blood caked on his face. I guess they were going for the dramatics.

They escorted me to the commander's office.

The commander never looked up once when we got inside. Ha, in your face King, you wore your makeup for no reason.

Sgt. King explained the situation, of course he left the part out where he was being racist and grabbed me. He painted me to be the bad person.

Only thing the commander heard was what happened during the mission. "So why didn't you shoot? Seems like all of this could have been avoided if you'd just done your job," he said, still not looking up.

"Sir they were kids, I may do anything for my job but kids is where I draw the line."

"You're fairly new so I understand but this is your job. With time it'll get easier."

Sgt. King was pissed that things weren't going his way. "I demand to press charges to the full extent. Anyone that tells someone that they'll skin them alive is a danger to society!"

The commander finally looked up, and something caught his attention. "He said what?"

King smiled. "Sir, he said he'll skin me alive."

Commander Busypants stared at me but spoke to Top, "Okay, I'll take it from here Captain. You and the QRF can return to your post."

That didn't sit too well with Top. "But sir, I'll be short a man and Khrist is my best gunner."

"Well take someone for Echo Team, they're going stateside in a week. I'm sure somebody will take some extra duty."

"With all due respect sir..."

The commander cut Captain Millman off. "That will be all Captain."

"Sir..."

"Unless you want to be picking up cigarette butts outside of the smoker's barracks on hands and knees, I suggest you and Barbie here head back to your dream house."

Barbie AKA King left first and Captain Millman followed with his head hung.

Commander Busypants was still eyeing me. "Where are you from, soldier?"

"St. Louis, Missouri, Sir," I answered.

His eyes went wide. "I'm General Moose, my unit calls me Knuckles. How would you like to run the operations of my unit?"

"Sir, I'm only an E-4, I'm not sure the soldiers would like being under the command of a lower enlisted."

"Enough of the formalities, just Knuckles. My soldiers are loyal, they'll follow the orders that I send down. You won't have any problems."

"I don't see a problem with at least giving it a try, Sir, I mean Knuckles. What would my duties be?"

As he picked up the phone he said, "You'll be heading up my crime division." Whoever he called answered. "Report to my office Sgt."

When the door swung open Sgt. Ghost AKA Dirty walked in. We shook hands.

Knuckles asked, "You two know each other already?"

Dirty took the question. "Of course Knuckles, he is a part of Al-Basra's QRF, Mr. Hawkeye himself."

"Was a part of, which is good because he had some experience with our op. I want you to train him in the leadership role of the division."

"And that would leave me where, I'm just curious?" Dirty asked.

"Supervision."

I don't know if I was lost in thought or a TV was on somewhere but I could have sworn that I heard a chicken.

"Y'all don't hear that?" I asked.

"Hear what?" they both asked at the same time.

"So neither of you hear a chicken clucking ?"

Knuckles broke out into laughter and pulled a cage from under his desk. "This here is my gamecock, his name is Dizzy."

Man it's some weird things going on around here. "Excuse me, but I'm a city boy, what do you need a chicken for?"

"Intimidation, soldier, intimidation."

"Ever since I've been a little boy I've always known for a chicken to be a symbol of fear, how do you intimidate with a chicken."

"I use it for interrogations, it helps me install fear into the person being interrogated. You grab it by the neck, hold its beak to the dirt and draw a line from its beak. That hypnotizes it and the insurgent believes we can hypnotize him so he speaks freely."

"I call bullshit," I said, not convinced.

"Come outside, I'll show you."

Knuckle held the chicken's nose to the ground and drew the line. It stayed dazed until he erased the line, then Dizzy became undizzy.

What in the chickity China the Chinese chicken shit was going on here?

"Sorry sir, but how exactly did you come up with this quote unquote magic trick?" I asked.

"Easy, experimentation."

"So you're just experimentally choking your chicken under your desk in your free time? Got it."

He looked at Dirty. "I think he'll fit right in with you guys."

"Roger that Knuckles, I'll get him introduced to the crew and throw him into action on tomorrow's run."

CHAPTER 28

Sgt. Dirty Ghost called a formation to introduce me to the unit. "Everyone remember Hawkeye from the QRF? Well he's going to be heading up our unit per Knuckles orders. I will be moving to supervisor, so if any questions were to come up, feel free to ask me and I'll send them up the chain to Specialist Khrist here," he said while pointing at me.

The unit roared, "HOOAH!"

Dirty introduced me to the squad leaders. "This is Alpha squad leader, Sgt. Pisser; Bravo squad leader, Sgt. Camel; Charlie squad leader, Sgt. Love Boat or LB for short and last but not least Delta's squad leader is Sgt. Giggles."

"What's with all the funny names around here?" I asked.

"I'm Pisser because I peed my pants the first mission that I went on with the division, Camel is named after Joe the Camel because he can't keep a cigarette out of his mouth, LB is always on the video with his girl trying to keep Jodie away and Giggles is the only one that laughs a Dirty's jokes."

What a bunch of weirdos.

"And I'm guessing Dirty gets his name because of his dirty jokes?" I asked.

"No, he's Dirty because of his mouth, let's just say cornhole is his favorite meal."

"So what's the deal with Knuckles, where'd he get his name from?"

Knuckles was standing at the door. "An old friend gave it to me when I first started with the division. That's all you need to know for the moment."

I asked him, "So Knuckles, I'm a little lost, why don't we use formalities in this unit?"

"Because we all work together to accomplish the mission. No one is greater than the next in my division."

"Copy that, I'm following, I believe."

"As time goes, you'll catch on. In the meantime you guys go get some rest, you have an early mission tomorrow. Dirty, show Hawkeye to the barracks and get him squared away. Hawkeye you'll retrieve your belongings tomorrow at the rendezvous with your old team," Knuckles instructed.

Dirty showed me to the sleeping quarters. "You want to hear a joke?" he asked.

"Sure, shoot," I answered, knowing that I should have declined. But what the hell, I didn't have too much to do anyway.

"So there was a couple that lived in a nursing home, when they were younger they would have sex everyday but as they got older the wife stopped being able to get wet. They sat at the picture window of the nursing home together everyday and the wife would hold the husband's cock in her hand to give him the sensation that he's being pleasured.

One morning she woke up and he was gone, she figured he went to breakfast early so she headed down. When she got there her heart was broken. The husband was sitting in their spot with his cock in another patient's hand. She screamed 'Tom what the hell is going on here?' and he answered, 'Oh Ann, she's got Parkinson's disease," he finished by cracking up.

I looked at him plainly. "I don't get it."

"She was jerking him off unintentionally because of the Parkinson's."

"That's sick as fuck, I see why they call you Dirty." I shook my head.

He laughed. "There's plenty more where that came from."

"I'm good, you can keep them where they're at," I declined.

After chow I retired to the barracks to check in with Tanner.

"Hello my beautiful Baby Love. You're looking extremely elegant today.

"I've been calling and emailing you all day, where the hell have you been? Y'all have never been out this long and you call me after every mission, I've been worried."

"I love it when you sound anxious about hearing from me. They assigned me to a new unit."

"Why, what was wrong with the other unit? I thought they needed you badly, that's why they expedited your deployment?" she inquired.

I explained to her about the fight with Sgt. King back on the QRF compound.

"Husband, you and your short fused attitude, you have to control your temper, especially over there. Everyone knows the military isn't color friendly, don't give them a reason to lose you over there."

"I'm not babe. I thought that too after I did it but when I got back here to Kuwait the commander here actually gave me a promotion for it. I'm leading the crime division now."

"That's not something that you see everyday."

"Exactly, well babe I gotta get some shut eye because if this is anything like the QRF I'm going to need all that I could get."

"You better learn to cat nap."

"Oh I have, and I will never make a joke about geriatric people and their thirty second naps ever again," I said seriously.

She laughed. "Okay. Love you Bae, I'll talk to you later."

"Love you more gorgeous."

CHAPTER 29

5AM and we were loaded and exiting the gates of Camp Arifjan. We met Captain Millman and the QRF at the rendezvous spot.

Dirty handed me the packet to give to Captain Millman.

I retrieved my belongings and gave him the package without an incident. The rest of the QRF acted like they didn't know me and I reciprocated.

"How'd it go?" Dirty asked when I mounted the HET.

"He seemed a little confused on how I was in control of the op after being reprimanded. I told him that his guess is as good as mine."

"He'll get over it unless he wants to pick boogers from suicide bombers noses."

I shook my head. "Are you always this dark?"

"Damn I thought I was white."

I'd had enough. "So what's the deal with this unit? Why don't we have any infantry vehicles attached to us instead of piggybacking QRFs?"

"I don't know, kid, that's how it's been since I've been here. My job was to do what you're doing now. I follow orders and go with the flow."

It took us three piggybacks to reach Herat and I had to deliver a package to every QRF Captain along the way.

We pulled into a container yard in the heart of Herat.

The place was crawling with nothing but insurgents and that made my skin start crawling too.

Dirty looked at me as I was making my weapon hot. "Easy kid, you won't be needing that."

"What, are you blind? Do you not see all of the bogies in here?" I asked with my finger on the trigger.

"We need to put you behind the wheel and out of the captain's seat so you won't be trying to shoot anybody. Just follow my lead and you'll be fine."

When we came to a stop we dismounted the vehicles. Me and Dirty walked over to the insurgent in charge.

"What's up Moe, this is Hawkeye. He'll be our new leader going forward. Today he's shadowing me, the next trip he'll be the guy."

Moe extended his hand, I shook it even though I was uneasy.

"Welcome aboard, Hawkeye, you have any questions please feel free to ask me. Dirty's got my SAT phone info, I'm always available to you," he said in a thick Arabic accent.

"One question, what are we shipping back and forth?"

He clapped me on the shoulder. "Now that is a question for Mr. Knuckles, I'm afraid I can't answer that one for you.

"Well what good are you?"

He laughed. "Let's get you guys unhooked and rehooked so you can be on your way."

Thirty minutes later we were headed back to camp. I was enjoying the position way more than I did with my QRF position.

***

Knuckles called me into his office when we got back to camp. "So what do you think? You like it so far?"

"It's smoother thank QRT and I'll be able to rest so I guess you can say that."

"That's good to hear, Friday's mission is the same except Moe will be sending back one of his men with you. You sure you can handle the position?"

"I'm sure, sir."

Friday before departing camp I decided I needed to figure out what was up. Time to have a look at the cargo.

All three trailers were filled with weapons and ammunition.

Why the hell are we giving weapons to our enemies?

Just do your job G.I. Joe.

***

"Hawkeye, what's smoking my man's?" Moe asked upon our arrival to the meeting spot.

"Not too much Moeski, Knuckles said we'll have one of your men riding back with us today. Where is he so we can get going?"

"He's already loaded up my friend."

I looked around. "Loaded where?"

"Follow me, I'll show you", he turned and started heading to the back of one of the trailers that we would be pulling back.

When he opened the trailer door there was a man of Arabic descent handcuffed in a cage. Behind him were bales of fentanyl.

I jumped back.

"You alright, Hawkeye?"

"Yea I'm straight, I didn't expect to see a man tied up. I thought he'd be leaving under his own free will."

He laughed as he closed the doors. "Knuckles still leaving you guys in the dark I see."

We swapped trailers and headed back to camp, I didn't say a word the entire ride. Dirty kept asking if I was cool, I wouldn't even respond.

Knuckles met us at the warehouse when we pulled back into the FOB.

My trailer was the first in but last to be unloaded. Knuckles, Dirty and myself unloaded it after he dismissed the rest of the unit.

The prisoner was taken out of the cage and we dragged him to a room that had a bunch of medical supplies. I figured that it was the torture chamber, WRONGO!

Knuckles hooked him up to an IV and hit him with a dose of anesthesia. When he went under Knuckles put a tool to hold eyes open in the insurgents eyes then he took another tool that looked like two spoons and pulled both of his eyes out of his sockets.

I almost lost my lunch. What the fuck did I get myself into?

Me and Dirty carried the unconscious Arab to a pit behind the warehouse. He had me help hogtie him to a pole then we placed the pole over the pit like a rotisserie.

Knuckles came out of the warehouse and gave the prisoner a shot of adrenaline. He started bucking against the pole like crazy when he regained consciousness because his world was plunged into total darkness without his eyes. He started yelling in Arabic.

Knuckles walked over to him and held the Arab's nose, when he opened his mouth for air Knuckles stuck his missing eyeballs in his mouth and taped it shut.

"Next time watch your mouth you piece of shit," Knuckles said tersely stepping out of the pit.

What he did next made my entire digestive system come out of my mouth.

He set the pit on fire and roasted the Arab like a rotisserie chicken.

I've smelt burned food before and that shit stinks but compared to burned human, burned food smells like the fragrance aisle in a department store.

The Arab was kicking and screaming. Every time he looked like he would pass out, Knuckles would hit him with another shot of adrenaline.

Fifteen minutes later, his legs and arms were melted to nubs and his body fell into the fire pit.

Only then did Knuckles allow him to die.

Dirty turned to me and said, "Clean yourself up and meet us in Knuckles office in ten."

CHAPTER 30

When I sat down at Knuckle's desk he handed me one of the packets that I gave to the QRF.

"What's this, do we have another mission? I thought we only ran twice a week."

"No, that's your payment for the week, open it up," he directed.

Inside were a hundred $100 bills.

"Ten thousand dollars, Knuckles am I supposed to split this within the unit?" I asked shockingly.

"Negative, that's your weekly payment for being a part of my unit. They'll get their own."

"This is a lot of money to make in a week, Knuckles, my first and fifteenth check is fine with me."

"You're so wet behind the ears. After your second trip of the week you'll receive your weekly bonus on top of Uncle Sam's pay."

"Sir, if I'm going to continue working for you, I'm going to have to get some answers out of you. First, I thought we were working to stop crime, not adding to it, we're trading weapons for dope. And what was that back there at the warehouse?" I demanded.

"I knew you'd be like your grandfather. Brightness must run in your family. That dumb fuck back there leaked the information to our route to some villagers that are against our agreement that we have with the locals."

Before he could get any further I interrupted him. "Did you say my grandfather? How do you know my grandfather?"

"This operation was set up and operated by your grandpa, Big Bank Frank."

"Naw no way, my grandfather was in an infantry unit or something," I said, showing my doubts.

"Well yes that was his MOS but like you're doing now, he did some extracurricular activities in the theater," he said spreading his arms and continued, "and this is it. When you were born he decided to leave it behind and I was his leader of the division so he left it to me."

He pulled out a SAT phone and dialed a number then handed it to me.

On the fifth ring Pop picked up. "Moose Knuckles, how's it going? My boy doing alright with the QRF over there?"

"No Pop, it's me," I said gloomily.

I heard him gasp and go quiet.

"Pop, tell me that Knuckles is lying. He's gotta be, right Pop?" I begged,

"Remember when I told you that I would take my military career to the grave with me? That's exactly what I was talking about. It's also the reason why I didn't want you going into the service. How did you get out of the QRF and into the CD?"

"First you're going to tell me if what Knuckles is talking about is true or not!" I demanded.

"He's still calling himself that, huh? I gave him that name, the kid was always crotch watching."

Pop filled me in on how he set up the operation to gain the trust of the locals and how it turned into an actual drug ring after stumbling upon a poppyseed farm.

I told him about the incident with King at the QRF and about Knuckles taking me in when they brought me to be reprimanded.

We spoke for a few minutes, he gave me some advice and then hung up.

Knuckles jumped straight in, "So now that that's out of the way, you staying?"

"If Pop started this then I think I'm in the right place but I only have about seven months left. I guess I can stick around until I depart."

"I'm sure you'll decide to stay after you see how much bread you'll be pulling in," Knuckles warned.

"Actually sir, I just recently married, my wife would have an aneurysm if I stayed over here longer than expected. She's already pissed that I deployed so soon after our wedding."

"I can understand that, well the offer will remain on the table if you ever change your mind. On to the next matter of business, in order for you to head up the CD, we have to get you promoted to a sergeant," Knuckles stated.

"Knuckles I've only been out of basic training for eight months, wouldn't I have to be in for at least three years in order for me to become a NCO?"

"When you have friends in high places vouching for you anything is possible. You'll have your rank by Monday. Go enjoy your weekend soldier."

Tanner was excited to hear that I had a better position with great pay. I left out the part about it being an illegal operation, I knew she'd flip her wig if I told her about that.

What she doesn't know won't hurt.

CHAPTER 31

For the remaining seven months I ran the drop and hook operation to the best of my ability.

Some things that I saw that could be improved I offered my opinion to Knuckles which we included in the day to day operations. One of the biggest suggestions was to attach a permanent assault squad to the CD. To keep them fresh and alert along the route we would have the gunners swap out at the original rendezvous locations. With that new squad we added two gun trucks, one that Dirty and I rode in and oh how I loved pressing buttons, that was more exciting than running the .50 cal.

Once we transitioned into the new and improved tactic, Knuckles added the saved $30,000 to my weekly bonus. I was up to $40,000 cash per week.

Every month I would send my earnings home in packages that I mailed to Tanner. She didn't ask too many questions after I told her I was getting bonuses for using my ninja capabilities.

In a way I was. Cue evil scientist laugh.

CHAPTER 32

Departure day stumbles upon me before I could blink an eye.

Knuckles called me into his office suggesting that we go ahead and get the elephant out of the room. He could tell that I knew something was up because I'd been avoiding him for a few weeks.

Before he could waste his breath I stopped him. "Knucks, I'm not staying over here, so you might as well not even ask me."

"Actually, I've come to the conclusion that I myself will be returning stateside as well. I've been here for thirty years now, I think it's time that I move on."

"So who's going to run the CD when you leave?"

Don't even think about it G.I. Joe, I thought to myself.

"I'm going to leave it to Dirty, the way Big Bank Frank did for me."

"So what, you're just going to retire, or are you taking command elsewhere?"

"First things first, if you think Frank isn't seeing money from this operation still, you're crazy," he said with a laugh. "Then secondly, that's what I wanted to talk to you about. I've been talking to your grandpa about trying to persuade you to stay and take over but he suggested that we move on from the stone ages and expand. He told me about the AAG and proposed that we turn them into an offspring of the CD. We'll have to train them but it's doable, what do you think?"

"I don't think my guys would want to drive convoys from state to state, we're more of a let's get active type of gang," I informed him.

"That's what we meant by expansion, the product that we get from Moe, instead of putting it on a flight to South or Central America, we bring it straight to the states. No cut, no re-rock. One hundred percent product."

"And how the hell are we supposed to sell all of this product?" I challenged.

"Wholesale, we cut out the cartels then we can drop the price. Quality and numbers sell in this business. We already have connections over there, I'll set it up to where they'll come straight through you," Knuckles answered smoothly.

"So we'll basically be an American drug hub?"

He pointed at me. "You catch on fast."

"What are the percentages?"

"Seventy percent of the profit is yours, the other thirty will be split by me and Frank. However you decide to split that between your guys is completely up to you. For the three month training period they'll be paid ten thousand a week. They'll get a one hundred twenty thousand dollar sign on bonus, with that they should be able to get appropriate living quarters and transportation. Make sure they lease everything and not buy out right. Frank told me about an old abandoned school named Simmons that's in the area. We'll turn that into our training facility and that'll be done within a month. When training is done, it'll be our permanent hub, questions?"

"Yeah, when does all of this go into effect, because I promised to take my wife on a honeymoon after my deployment."

"That wouldn't be a problem, the completion of the training facility won't be done for another month. Frank has been there overseeing the project since we concocted the idea six months ago."

"Y'all just went ahead with plans like y'all knew I was going to say yes. What if I would have said no?"

"Then the last thing you would have seen was the fire pit as your body fell towards it after your limbs melted away," he threatened.

A chill ran down my back as I had a flashback of the Arab that we roasted after my first trip.

"What's the deal with that anyway?" I asked when I composed my nerves.

"That's something Frank taught me when I was sitting in the chair you're sitting in now. All the greats have a signature torture technique."

"There's no way Pop used to roast people to death."

"No, he gave me the idea. His signature was to cut a slit in their belly and pull their large intestine out and put it in their mouth so they could taste the shit that they talked."

"You motherfuckers are sick," I exclaimed, barely keeping my bile down.

"Well if you want to be great then you better get used to it. Frank made me sit there and shoot out ideas. None of mine sounded good so he suggested the rotisserie idea. So come on, let's hear what you got."

"Uh, I guess since I'm taking over my grandfather's op, I'll pay some homage to him. What about actually skinning someone alive? And I'll even incorporate a symbol of your method, I like the idea of the adrenaline to make sure that they live through the whole process," I suggested.

Knuckles' mouth dropped. "That gave me the damn jitters to just think about it. Remind me to never fuck with anybody in y'all family. After I tried five times I gave up. You nailed it on the first attempt. You have a lot of the notorious Frank in you, kid. We're going to great heights."

"Like you said, I catch on fast, after my first experience with the roast pit, I started to hatch my own little maneuver," I said as I rubbed my hands together.

He shook his head. "Now down to the last detail of this new op. I'm finding the facility and warehouse but you have to fund the three million for the start up."

His statement shocked me to the core. "Three million? Where the hell am I supposed to get that type of money? I haven't even made a million yet."

"Well you're a bright kid, I'm sure you'll put something together. You have approximately four months to put it together. As a matter of fact make it two months, that way we can perfect it in the last two months of training."

Still stunned, I asked, "What if I can't find that type of money, could we put our money together? That'll be roughly two point two mill."

"Three million is the number. That covers transporting and the product. Besides, the earnings from training are to be put towards exactly what we've already discussed."

"Okay, I'll talk to my guys and see what we can come up with. I can't make any promises though, that's a lot to come up with. It ain't like we can sell three million dollars worth of candy bars in two months."

"I have faith in you, you'll pull it off. If you don't have any more questions, I'll see you in a month."

"Just one more question, where would you suggest we go for a honeymoon?" I asked as I stood up.

He put his hands behind his head, he leaned back in his chair and smiled.

CHAPTER 33

It took me a week to get back to St. Louis. While I was enroute, I sent out a mass text to the AAG group chat: URGENT MEETING, need everybody to be present Sunday at noon at Simmons Elementary.

Gwalla and Banga would have to be present through FaceTime since they were still in Atlanta.

Next I called Tanner. "Love, I'll be home Friday evening, Monday morning we'll be flying out to our honeymoon."

"We haven't even chosen a new place to go, I thought we canceled Hawaii?"

"Just be packed come Monday morning, okay? I'm sure you'll be satisfied with the location *I* chose for us," I said putting an emphasis on I.

"How am I supposed to know how to pack if I don't know where I'm going?" Tanner shot back.

"Dress for all occasions, boo. Make sure you pack some good swimwear too."

My last call was to a friend that I knew was practicing to be a world renowned chef. I asked her if her and a friend of choice wanted to go on an all expenses paid two week vacation. When she accepted the offer I sent her all of the information she needed to book the flight.

Upon arrival at the airport Tanner was there to pick me up. She had a brand new set of wheels.

"Damn Bae, that Tesla Plaid looks really good on you," I said while hugging her.

"I'm a boss man's wife, I have to look the part, my love."

"You know you're so spoiled, right?"

"Well you made me this way," Tanner said while on her tiptoes giving me a kiss.

"I know. And for the record, you already looked the part from day one. Let's get home, I'm dying to see what you've done with the place. You got me all to yourself until Sunday."

"Why, what's Sunday?" she asked as we were getting into the car.

"I have a meeting with the gang."

"About?"

"Just a lil' business proposition, nothing too major. Sumn' slight buck a right."

She side eyed me and put her foot on the gas.

As we pulled into our driveway Tanner pressed the garage opener and a black G-Wagon Brabus was parked inside with a red bow on the hood.

I eyed her as we got out of her car. "What's this?"

She hugged me around the waist and looked up at me. "My gift to show you how grateful I am for everything that you do for us. This is my wedding gift to you. I love you,

Husband." she said as she landed a juicy kiss right on my lips.

A G-Wagon? Whoa, I knew I had to lay the dick down proper on her for that.

"I love you too, Mrs. Khrist."

We walked in the house and I instantly smelled the aromas from the kitchen. Tanner suggested that I check out the rest of the house first.

Every part of the house exceeded my expectations.

"I love what you did with the house and it feels warm, why is this room next to our's locked though?" I questioned after realizing that I couldn't get in there at first.

"Because that's the room I wanted to show you last," she said as she unlocked the door and opened it. "This is our own little playroom. All the things you're into, I incorporated them here. My personal favorite is this," she pressed a button and the wall between the rooms slid up and exposed a glass window that looked into the bedroom. "This is for when I want to watch or be watched," she cooed.

I realized that I was looking at a full blown sex dungeon. There was a wall with a glory hole in it, a milking table in the middle of the room, whips, tethers, chains and swings. The whole fucking nine, literally. Tanner was tapping into my inner pornstar.

"What did I ever do to deserve you?" I kissed her and started trying to undress her.

She stopped me. "Not yet babe, we have to eat first."

When we walked into the kitchen Day was cooking in nothing but some lace lingerie.

I turned to Tanner. "I know I said she can stay but is she going to be walking around like this all the time? I don't know how much temptation I'll be able to fight."

Tanner smiled. "She's our's, feel free to fuck her as you please. I always wanted to have a sex slave."

My mouth dropped and she closed it for me and added, "Just don't fall in love, that's my only condition."

I won't but I'm not so sure my joint won't, I thought to myself.

"I'm at a loss for words right now, this is unbelievable," I said.

"Well believe it baby, you give me the world so I'll give you the universe."

Dinner was excellent, Day cooked baked macaroni and cheese, steak, lobster, Caesar salad and ranch seasoned breadsticks filled with mozzarella cheese.

A feast for kings.

After dinner I showered, I had to wash the Middle East stank off of me. Then I went and fucked my women, royally.

CHAPTER 34

The gang and I all pulled up together on Sunday at noon. Everybody was gawking at the G-Wagon.

My little brother, Eyes, said, "If the Army pays you well enough to have one of these, sign me up now!"

Hit the breaks kiddo.

"You have to have a diploma or GED to join the Army, Mr. Dropout," I said, killing his dreams.

"Man, school is too boring."

"That's okay because I got something better than the Army. Y'all see this building? They're in there turning it into a training facility for us, it'll be finished in a month."

Shoota shouted, "The fuck we being trained for?"

"To start our own empire," I answered.

He laughed. "We don't need training to sell no drugs. We already do this shit everyday. We were born into this lifestyle."

"Not on this scale, everyone of us will have our own product to slang and we will only be selling wholesale. No cut, no breakdowns, straight keys."

Deuce laughed and said, "G.I. Joe, you expect us to believe that? I thought you were an Army man now?"

A black GMC Sierra Denali with blacked out windows pulled up into the school parking lot.

Knuckles hopped out.

"How did you get here so fast, and how did you know about this meeting?" I was confused.

"Remember what I told you, when you have friends in high places anything is possible. Me being here at your meeting is coincidental," Knuckles answered.

"Coincidence or not, I'm glad you showed up, they were just about to depart because they thought I was lying."

He laughed and started explaining the whole ordeal to them. Twenty minutes later he was wrapping it up.

When he told them about coming up with the startup Fatt Rell said, "Three million? Where the hell are we going to come up with that?"

It was my turn to laugh. "That's exactly what I said but we'll have to think of something. We have two months to come up with a plan. Even if I have to find a plan on my own, we're going to pull it off. This is an opportunity of a lifetime, this isn't something that we can pass up."

Shoota asked, "So the military is just a large drug operation?"

Knuckles answered quickly, "No, only my division which was created by Big Bank Frank. I'm assuming that you all know him as Khrist's grandpa."

Everybody looked at each other in total disbelief.

"It's true y'all, I talked to Pop about it myself. How y'all think I'm able to pull up in a G-Wagon, and this ain't the regular joint, this a Brabus. That muhfucka cost at least four hundred! Shit y'all see Tanner's car. Y'all will receive ten thousand a week until y'all complete the training stage. Then we'll move on to the operation of our choosing to raise the three mill. After that this facility will become our central warehouse. The classrooms on the fourth floor have been converted into lofts for you to live during training. Food and drinks will be prepared by the facility. When you have company they will only be allowed on the fourth floor, no exceptions! The bottom three will be off limits to them and they're only allowed after training hours," I told them.

"Seems like you have it under control. If you'll excuse me, I'm going inside to check on the progress," Knuckles said leaving our congregation.

I turned to the guys. "Y'all ready to run up a bag or what?"

Everybody agreed and yelled, "Hell yeah!"

"Bet that up. I'm going on my honeymoon for two weeks so I'm three weeks I'll see y'all back here. Get ready, this shit comes fast and our world is about to go in a direction we would have never imagined. AAG is about to not only run city but the country."

"A's up or Al's up till my days up!" we all said in unison.

Before I left the city and headed home I decided to stop at my mom and Pop's house.

Fox, my mom's boyfriend, was on the porch.

"What's up fat boy, where is my mom and Pop?" I asked as I walked onto the front porch.

"You always got the jokes, huh? They're in the house. What's up, how's the military treating you? I see you pulling up in Brabuses and shit."

I laughed. "That's Tanner's doing bro, she got it as a wedding gift for me."

It just dawned on me that Fox drives trucks and he used to be connected with the cartel until he went to jail for a seven year stint. He always had some scheming type of lick going on.

"Aye Fox, let me ask you something, if you had to come up with three million, how would you do it?"

I saw a spark in his eyes before he spoke. "Me personally, I would go after those no-good pieces of shit motherfuckers that set me up. Why, what do you need three million for? I know Tanner ain't sucking you dry like that, is she?"

I laughed out loud. "Nah man, I got offered a proposition of a lifetime and the startup fee is three mill."

"Sounds illegal," he mused.

"Very illegal, but with legal backing."

"Tell you what, let me in on the operation side of things and I may be able to get you that three mill, plus a few."

"If you promise to keep it between us, you got a deal. But you don't know what I'm doing," I said after a second thought.

"I was just about to tell you the same thing. If there's a three mill buy in then I can only imagine the return," Fox said.

We shook on it and went into the house.

Pop was in the kitchen picking greens and baking some hot water cornbread. For some reason, dinner was always done by 3PM in Pop's household, and they always wondered why I was stealing snacks. I was hungry dammit.

"Look what the wind blew in, what's up Sergeant New and Improved CD?" Pop teased.

"What's up, Pop?" I asked giving him a hug.

"You know, just whipping up a little Sunday dinner. It's more than enough if you want to stay, Knuckles will be joining us after a while," he offered.

"Nah, I gotta get back home, we're going out of the country in the morning."

"Deploying again huh? I thought you were going to run the division here?"

"I'm taking Tanner on a nice honeymoon for a couple of weeks. I'll be staying in town a while after that. Knuckles told me that you helped hatch the plan to bring the CD to the states so that I could be here with my family and friends. You didn't have to do that, Pop, I've made enough money to be comfortable with a regular military job."

He waved me off. "You have to think big, son, I hear you're a natural. I want you to be better than I ever was. My biggest priority is your welfare and one day you'll have to take care of us older folks around here. You can't do that with a little military job."

"My well being? Pop you know Knuckles would have turned me into a shish kabob if I would have declined? And why the heck do you call him Moose Knuckles?"

"Believe me, he wouldn't have done that, he wouldn't have wanted to taste his own shit. I gave everybody code names in my unit in case we were intercepted over the radio, nobody would know who we were. His last name was Moose and the boy couldn't keep his eyes off the women's pussy prints," Pop said, shaking his head.

"Man y'all are sinister. How come you never told me about the CD, Pop? I would have understood, especially growing up around here."

"I wanted that way of life as far as possible from this family. I believe in the saying, that what's meant to be will be and that what isn't meant to be, won't. You found the CD on your own so in my opinion, it was meant for you."

"Thank you, Pop. I better get going before I have an angry wife after me."

"You sure you don't want to stick around for dinner?" he offered again.

I put my hand on his shoulder. "Pop, I have a personal chef now, I think I'll be eating a lot more home cooked meals now."

"Living the high life now huh?"

"I only learned from the best."

On the way out I spoke to earlybody and told Fox we'll link up when I get back in town.

CHAPTER 35

My lovely wife went shopping for our vacation and had all of our luggage packed by Sunday evening. Monday morning Day drove us to the airport in the G-Wagon because we had too much luggage for Tanner's Tesla.

I checked us into our flight without Tanner because I wanted her to be surprised when we walked up to our departure gate.

She lost her shit when she saw that our flight was destined for Italy.

"You put all of this together for me? Where are we going to be staying?" she asked me following a long kiss.

"This is all you get for now, General Moose told me about this place. I looked it up and knew you'd love it. See, husbands can be good for something," I winked.

"Italy is beautiful, I can't wait."

"Not as beautiful as you, though."

"You always know the right things to say at the right times."

"Because I'm a smooth operator," I sang aloud.

Somewhere over the Atlantic Ocean I woke up to my dick being pulled out of my pants.

Tanner started sucking it right there in the seat without a care in the world.

It was the middle of the day so the plane was filled with light. Luckily the people seated around us were sleeping and I was in the window seat.

She sucked me off the bone until I came all down her throat. She didn't waste a drop.

"Come on, let's go to the bathroom, my pussy is throbbing," Tanner whined.

"Babe, behave," I demanded.

"Don't be a bitch, come fuck me right damn now!"

And that's exactly what I did, I bent her ass over the sink in the rear bathroom and beat her inside until she had Bambi legs.

She woke some of the people up that were closest to the bathroom with her moaning so they eyeballed us when we walked back to our seat.

An older couple smiled and the wife said, "Welcome to the mile high club."

CHAPTER 36

We went straight to the AirBnb and crashed when we finally landed in Italy. I had jet lag bad or should I say Tanner lag.

The next morning I rolled over and Tanner wasn't on her side of the bed. There wasn't a note with $40 dollars in it either so I knew she couldn't have gone too far.

I got up and went looking for her.

The doors to the living room balcony were wide open. Tanner was standing against the rail looking out at the Gulf of Salerno. Her nakedness made me crave her.

I crept up on her and kneeled down quietly and stuck my tongue in her ass. My index and middle finger played with her pearl tongue.

After she exploded I came up for air. "Welcome to the Amalfi Coast, Mrs. Khrist," I said while kissing her neck.

Still moaning she said, "It's so beautiful, Husband."

"Now that you've told me how you look, what do you think about the view?"

"Stand up and I'll show up."

She slid my dick into her pussy and fucked me back as I fucked her. All while we looked out at the gulf.

The town we stayed in was built into the cliff overlooking the gulf and it was a sight to see.

Tanner and I went to explore the beach after we got cleaned up and dressed.

I texted Chef Jazz to let her know that I wanted dinner to be done at 5PM and she gave me the okay.

My stomach started growling so hard that we decided to eat lunch at Stella Maris, an Italian restaurant on the beach. I realized that I hadn't eaten anything since leaving the states except Tanner's ass.

The view of the gulf and the amount of yachts amazed Tanner. She whined until I finally conceded into booking a short private charter. They gave us a tour of the coastal line, they took us into the natural caves and scuba diving.

When it was time for us to return to shore the captain gave me his personal number and told us he would be more than happy to personally take us on different excursions while we were in the area.

As soon as we walked through the door Tanner looked at me. "What did you do?"

Chef Jazz set up a dining table lit by candles on the balcony that seated two. I escorted Tanner to her seat and Jazz brought out our platters which consisted of Tuscan creamy chicken, mostaccioli, a salad and breadsticks. She served us red wine to complete the meal.

I wanted crab legs instead of the chicken because I knew that it was an aphrodisiac but Jazz let me know that they didn't match with pasta.

She insisted on staying to clean up when we were done but I told her that I would handle it. We set a schedule to cook our three meals per day then she left.

I turned my attention back to Tanner.

"So you put this together all by yourself?" she questioned.

"All by myself," I said.

"Where'd you find an American chef over here?"

"She's a service member that went through basic with me, she didn't like it so she dropped out and took up culinary arts. I arranged to have her and a friend to stay over for two weeks to be your personal chef. She was more than excited to add this to her professional catalog."

"This is amazing, all of it. The whole surprise location, the view, the chef, the yacht and especially the way you ate my ass this morning. What's gotten into you?" Tanner asked playfully.

"I feel like I was abandoning you when I went overseas plus I can't pull all my tricks out at once, you'll get bored fast," I teased.

"Oh is that right? Well what tricks do you have in the bag for me now?"

"Who says I have any tricks to pull out right now?"

"Your eyes, I can tell by the way you're looking at me."

"How about you come over here so that I can show you," I instructed.

Tanner stood up and walked around the table seductively, I hoisted her up and sat her on the table. I tucked my lap towel around my neck like a bib, lifted her dress and devoured her while I sat in the chair.

She threw her head back and moaned, "I thought you just ate a full course meal, how do you still have room to eat?"

"There's always room for dessert, boo."

She came, I carried her into the bedroom room and ate her over and over until she passed out from climaxing too much.

CHAPTER 37

At 9AM Jazz had French toast, eggs, turkey bacon and apple juice made to serve.

"So Jazz, who'd you come with, a friend or your beau?" Tanner asked while we were finishing up our breakfast.

I side eyed her. "Babe, stop flirting, we're not having your shenanigans on this vacation, Jazz is here for business."

Jazz responded anyway, "It's okay, I'm used to this and Mrs. Khrist, I'm here with my beau."

Tanner snapped at me, "I wasn't flirting, I was going to extend an invitation to Jazz and her partner to enjoy an evening of yachting with us. I'm sure they're tired of being cooped up in their room all day."

"Actually, that's a great idea. How about it, Jazz?" I asked with intentions to ease the mood.

"Well I did bring a few swimsuits, I think I'll take you up on that offer," Jazz answered after a quick thought.

Did I just see Tanner licking her lips?

I leaned over and whispered, "We are not about to become swingers, chill."

We met at the dock and I half expected to see a tall basketball type of man with Jazz. That was not the case, she had a fine brown skinned Brazilian woman with her. Both of them were wearing the shit out of their swimsuits.

Jazz introduced her lady friend as Taz. Jazz and Taz, go figure.

We set sail and Tanner asked me, "You like what you see, huh?"

"Yeah, kinda," I admitted.

"I figured you would."

"What does that mean?" I asked, confused.

"I clocked them on the flight. I wanted to run into them anyway, just so happens they were here with us by chance. You're not the only one with tricks up your sleeve," Tanner said, sticking out her tongue.

"And here I was thinking that I was the horn dog."

The two weeks went by super fast. We went to the sea everyday. The yacht Captain took us jet skiing, rafting, diving, parasailing and to do a bunch of other water activities.

Jazz and Taz joined us everyday and they brought strawberries. They were super fun, both on the yacht and the bedroom.

I couldn't make this up, I was having an orgy with three bad women, all with banging bodies. What more could a man ask for on his honeymoon.

My mood was a little somber when we flew out of Italy, it was time to get back to reality and the money. I loved both but what I was leaving behind was depressing.

CHAPTER 38

We arrived at the airport in St. Louis, Jazz told us to give her a call any time that we would need her services and thanked us for a grand time.

Day had the G-Wagon washed and detailed when she picked us up.

I was living one hell of a life.

Tanner and Day climbed into the back seat and locked into the 69 position so I jumped behind the wheel.

While we were on our honeymoon I explained my new situation to Tanner. At first she didn't like it but after I ran down the events of the last year and that it was Pop's original operation, she softened up to the idea. She only had one condition, that I confide in her before we launch the drug operation and I don't ever hold anything back from her again.

After I dropped the girls off I headed straight to the hood. Everybody was outside posted up. The offer that I made to them was so good that everybody dropped out of college to run up a check. They were enjoying the last few days of their freedom. I can't say that I blamed them, why get further into debt when they can get rich quick?

My boy Sanchez was the first to greet me. "G.I. Joe, the fuck is up, gang? How was the honeymoon?"

"All I can tell you is strawberries and baddies bro. If I told you, you probably wouldn't even believe half of it."

"Knowing you and Tanner, with y'all freaky asses anything is possible. You came up with any ideas to get the three yet? We've been thinking about a few bank jobs, like the LAB boys did when we were younger."

"That shit too messy and too many things can go wrong at any time. You seen Set It Off," I asked him, attempting to get him to see that his logic was off.

"C'mon gang, that's the movies. So what idea did you come up with, Mr. Clean?"

"Yeah and this is real life with real life time and real life death. I'm about to run in here and talk to Fox, he might be able to help us.

"Your mom's boyfriend?"

"Yeah, him gang."

"Man dude been out of the game a long time. Plus he was just a truck driver, he ain't goin' know too much," Sanchez shot back.

"When someone sets you up to take the fall, you have a lot of time to do research and plan a revenge. I'll see what he says and run it by Knuckles, then we'll go from there. If all else falls then we'll go with y'all messy ass plan."

"Bet that," he said as we shook on it.

I dapped everybody up and went to my childhood home.

Pop was in the backyard cleaning some fish and running the grill at the same time. He looked happy when he saw me come through the gate.

"What's up Pop? Are you sure you are cleaning those fish well enough?" I teased.

"Son, I taught you how to clean fish, what makes you think the student is better than the teacher? Knuckles told me about your choice of torture, you know if I didn't know any better, I'd say you're shaping up to be just like me, boy," he said with a smile.

"I guess you can say that. You know where Fox is?"

"He's right there under the hood of that slow ass Mustang. Don't know what your mom sees in him, real men drive Chevy."

Ever since I've known Fox he's been a racing fanatic and he thought his 2004 Cobra was faster than a rocket putting a man on the moon.

"What up, Fox?"

He bumped his head on the hood of his suckstang. "What up man," he asked, rubbing his head.

"Not too much, just got back from the Amalfi Coast about an hour ago."

"Italy huh, how was it?"

Strawberries and baddies bruh, strawberries and baddies," I said looking off into the distance.

"I'll take it that you had a good time."

"Take it as a pleasurable time! So what's up, have you put something together yet?"

"Actually I did. But before I explain it to you, I need you to know that these are extremely dangerous people and things might get hairy. Are you sure that you want to go up against that?"

"Fox, you've known me for ten years now, you know me and the guys don't duck no wreck. As long as we plan for everything we'll be straight."

"Just had to be sure, that's all."

He ran through his idea and how we would have to get it. He took it upon himself to make sure that it was still a good lick while I was out of the country.

"So how much are we talking?" I asked.

"Between seven and ten."

"Damn, that's a good measure and I thought you were just a dumb truck driver," I joked.

"That's fucked up man."

We both laughed.

Knuckles liked the plan so well that he extended an offer to Fox to join us in training since he would be needed to execute the plan.

CHAPTER 39

Training kicked off and Knuckles had me help with the task. It was just like basic; classroom, exercise, eat and repeat. Only difference was it was more fast tracked since we only had a month to train the fundamentals. The last two months would be strictly mission training.

The crew did an amazing job so at the end of the week Pop and Knuckles threw a big BBQ for everyone.

Monday came around and it was time to learn how to operate weapons.

I know what you're thinking, why put military grade weapons in the hands of a bunch of gangsters? Let me be the bearer of bad news, that's military trained gangsters. We don't hold our handguns sideways and our rifles at our waist when we fire. Neither do we do drive-bys, we walk up, aim, squeeze and execute.

The basement of the facility was turned into an indoor shooting range that was available to use for training purposes whenever we needed.

Being around guns for most of our lives was a plus. They were already familiar with the basic mechanics. All we had to teach them was proper breathing and steadiness. The other fundamentals were second nature.

Everybody picked up on the training so well that the first month flew past.

The next phase was simple, figuring out who would be doing what in the operation after we got the three million dollars secured. Classroom work was normally boring but that day it was completely different.

Knuckles stood in front of the class. "Today we're going to pick your new professions, who would like to go first? No matter what it is, we're going to have it."

Eyes was the first with his hand up. "I want to be a professional assassin."

The class erupted in laughter.

I thought for a second. "That's actually not a bad idea," I started catching everybody off guard. "We all can't be drug savvy, someone has to have some clean money and someone has to have the dirty money, that way we can keep all the washing in-house. So how about this, if someone picks a drug profession, the next person picks a legit profession. That way we keep the majority of our spending in-house as well."

Remember as kids, we all had that question: what do I want to be when I grow up? Well this is how dreams begin my friends.

Everybody went around and made their decision.

Deuce: Heroin
Big Money: Car dealer
Animal: Marijuana
Peezy: Real Estate

Sanchez: Fentanyl

Lazy: Lazy for legal businesses

Stuck: Security for illegal business

Relex: Cocaine and crack

Reddot: Strip Club

Gwalla and Banga: Activities for Atl

Fox: Transportation and logistics

Fatt Rell and Borey wanted to be rappers so we let them have that as both of their professions.

That left Shoota and myself.

I would oversee the finances and the product flow. Shoota was to take care of the day to day operations, he would set up the transactions of the illegal structure.

From the sounds of it we had a well oiled machine.

On to the next order of business, the heist preparations.

Fox and Knuckles instructed the class on how we were going to carry out the plan.

The first half of the day we would go to the classroom to study, the second half we practiced the routine and maneuvers.

It got to the point where we could operate the drill in our sleep and that's just how it had to be. There was no room for mistakes, an oops could be disastrous.

The week before the actual heist we ran two dry runs. The first one only a few things were botched. The second run was flawless. Everybody was familiar with all pieces of the puzzle.

Normally the weekends were ours to enjoy but with the heist so close, Knuckles and I thought it would be best to keep everyone in the facility so that we wouldn't have anybody getting too lit and going AWOL before the heist.

On Sunday everyone had their game faces on. We left the facility at noon in a fast paced convoy to get to set up on our positions until it was time to strike.

My last lecture before we departed was, "Stay alert, keep your head on a swivel and communicate. Last but not least, hit it hard and fast!"

"A's up or K's up till my days up!"

Sanchez hit the designated airwaves, "The Angel has passed Muskogee, target is right on schedule for receiving."

Big Money picked up next, "Angel received and saved."

Fox used to be a transporter for the Gato Cartel, he ran their product between Laredo, Texas and Kansas City, Missouri three times a week.

Eight years ago the Gato Cartel had set him up to get caught by the DEA. They worked a deal that if the cartel let the DEA catch one of their shipments a year then the other 155 would get through untouched.

Unfortunately it was Fox's run that they bartered with. Fortunately for us, Fox knew the exact trucks and routes used by the cartel to transport their merchandise.

When he was running for them Sunday nights would be the run to transport seven million cash at the least, from Kansas City to Laredo for the week. They would trade off trailers and he'd start his mule run for the week.

Our target was in sight of the second leg team of our operation.

The truck came rolling through Dallas on Interstate 635 Relex picked up the trail.

Big Money would fall back and wait at that spot and wait on our return.

We had to take the pedal to the metal before the load hit Laredo.

Relex spoke over the earwig. "The Angel is thirty minutes from church."

"Copy, church doors are open for service. Stay sharp, if the Angel gets too close to Nuevo Laredo the devil will accept it with open arms," Fox responded.

The Angel was the codename for the load, church was code for the interception spot and the devil was code for the Gato Cartel.

We were set up ten minutes before the city of Laredo, Texas. When the truck was within sight Borey was to have a breakdown in the middle of the highway, Eyes, Stuck and Animal were to stall the other lanes by stopping and helping to 'fake push' him out the way.

Once traffic was clogged up Shoota, Deuce and myself were to hold the 'Angel' at gunpoint to make sure he didn't radio back to the cartel.

Fox still had the master key to all the trucks so while we had the driver frozen he would unlock the door and we'd climb in. The driver was put into the sleeper where Deuce and Shoota kept their guns trained on him.

Fox got behind the wheel and I jumped shotgun.

I called over the airwaves, "Angel has been baptized."

That was our signal to get traffic moving along.

Fox had a spot in Austin where we stashed the bobtail that we would switch the trailer to before we headed back home.

Peezy stayed there with the truck to make sure nobody investigated it. He was sitting in the cab of the truck when we reached the swap spot.

The driver that we had hostage was bargaining for his life. "There's two sicarios in the trailer that guard money while it's in transport."

Fox saw the way I looked at him. "Don't worry, I knew about them and I planned for it. That's why I stuck the signal jammer on the trailer before we took off."

"Bro, what! What if we would have had to replace you or something happened to you before the mission?" I exclaimed.

"I couldn't have chanced y'all not allowing me to get some get back. I got this," he smiled.

"So what you got in mind?" I asked after calming down.

He turned to the shaken up driver. "You want to live to see your family again?"

The driver nodded.

"Well you're going to walk back here with us and signal to the sicarios that you've made it to the Laredo rendezvous. If you warn them that something is wrong, I'll drag you all the way to the border tied to the trailer itself."

The driver agreed.

I asked Fox, "So you don't know the code or did you forget it?"

"They change it every drop for safety precautions like this." He pulled a stun grenade out of his cargo pocket. "Let's hit 'em hard and raw, or whatever you said."

We approached the back of the trailer with the driver eating the barrel of Deuce's pistol.

He did the code, which was four knocks, hand slide followed by seven quick raps.

A lock was unsecured from the inside of the trailer and we all looked at each other.

Fox mouthed for me to unlock the door latch. He pulled the pin on the stun grenade when I opened the door enough he threw it through the crack and I slammed it shut.

We all hit the dirt and covered our ears.

A fusillade of bullets came ripping through the trailer door then the stun grenade went off and the shooting stopped.

We were up and through the door instantly before the sicarios could recover. They both were in the fetal position with their hands gripping their ears. They were zip tied and thrown out of the trailer into the dirt.

Fox took off his ski mask after we got them to their knees.

"Yo what the fuck are you doing, bro? Stick to the plan, you've already deviated enough," I screamed at him.

"I want these motherfuckers to see that they fucked over the wrong amigo," Fox responded while giving them a dark death stare.

"That's going to bring heat down on the whole operation, man. Fuck!" I was passed stressed. It's a good thing that we were behind an abandoned warehouse.

"Yeah you're right, it would if they were going to live to see tomorrow," Fox stated calmly.

He pulled out two .38 snub nosed revolvers and looked both sicarios in the eyes as he pulled the trigger, killing them both execution style.

I pointed to the shivering driver. "So now what about him? You showed your face and they'll beat him within an inch of his life until they get the answers that they need."

He looked at the driver. "You held up your end, I'll hold up my end. You didn't see anything here tonight right, Dennis?"

"No," said Dennis, the shivering driver.

Fox instantly raised his gun and shot him in between the eyes. "Good, now you can't tell God what I've done." He drew a cross over himself with his hand.

Dude seriously, what kind of people did I surround myself around, I thought to myself.

We detached the trailer from their bobtail and hooked it up to the one that we brought. The recently deceased were placed into their bobtail and the entire inside was doused with bleach and ammonia to kill any evidence of us. Then it was set on fire.

Peezy, Reddot, Borey, Stuck, Eyes and Jizzle all surrounded the Angel to keep a lookout for followers.

Relex was in Dallas with Big Money so when we came rolling through they fell into formation as well, two lead vehicles, two on each side of the Angel and two taking up the rear.

I felt like I was back in the Middle East running with the CD again.

Once we hit Muskogee we had to come to a single file convoy. Sanchez fell in line a mile ahead to ensure that the route was clear.

From Joplin back to St. Louis it was smooth sailing.

CHAPTER 41

The crew was dismissed when we pulled back into the facility. It was a full day since anybody had gotten any real sleep. They were exhausted and I couldn't say that I blamed them. I remembered my first mission and how tired I was.

Knuckles met me at the warehouse while Fox backed the trailer up to the dock. He came inside with me and Knuckles when he finally got the trailer into the dock.

I pulled him to the side. "Bro, I know you wanted your vengeance but that clusterfuck back there that you pulled was out of control. Pull something like that again and we'll have a real problem. I can't have people going rogue when they feel like it," I threatened.

"I know, I should have brought the situation to light but I needed there to not be any obstacles in the way of getting my payback."

"We could have planned for that, bro."

We agreed and proceeded to inspect the trailer. It had a false wall installed so that if you opened the door all you saw were stacked boxes.

We let Fox have the honor of opening the wall since he had experience with that kind of stuff. Inside were pallets of stacked bills.

Gwalla and Banga unloaded the trailer with forklifts that were left over from the construction of the facility. It took them half an hour to get all of the pallets out of the trailer and into the warehouse's shipping area. There were twenty six pallets in total.

The last part of the last part of the heist was to reassemble the tracker on the trailer and ditch it before they located it.

My cousin Tony was always looking for a quick buck and he had his CDL so I paid him ten thousand to drive the trailer to Memphis and abandon it.

No questions asked he went on his merry little way.

It took us three days to run and rerun all twenty six pallets through the money counters. Me, Knuckles and Fox alternated running the machine, day in and day out.

The total came up to $250,000,000. That's why we reran the counters because we thought they were broken the first time the total came out.

I looked at Fox crossly after we confirmed the amount. "I thought you said seven to ten million."

"Back when I was running it, it was maybe fifteen max. These motherfuckers have upgraded big time and think about it, this is every Sunday."

"Damn, that's a lot of dinero," I said, sounding dumbfounded.

Knuckles laughed. "That's chump change compared to the amount of revenue that we'll be bringing in."

Fox's eyes went wide. "Damn, ain't no way. That's a lot of paper."

Me and Knuckles both laughed.

Instead of the original three million we tripled the startup amount. All the product was to be delivered straight to the warehouse in three weeks, Fox and Knuckles would work that part of logistics out. Moe said he needed that much more time since it was triple the original agreement.

We gave Fox $40,000,000 since he was the one that set up the heist. The remaining $200,000,000 was all mine, muha-ha-ha.

Just kidding, I wanted my guys to be rewarded for their parts in the heist so I gave them an extra $500,000 on top of the $120,000 they earned for training. The rest would be used to invest into the legit businesses.

I decided to take the whole gang on vacation while we waited for the three weeks to pass, they deserved it.

CHAPTER 42

"Yo Mike, it's Keefer, Todd's nephew. Look man, I'm going to be in town for about two weeks, can you make something happen for me?" I asked over the phone.

Mike was one of the owners of a hotel named The Clevelander on South Beach. My uncle, the late and great Rodd, turned the Cleve into a beachfront party hotel over the last two decades.

"Yo what's up brother? For one of Rodd's boys I'll make anything happen, that's no question. What size room are you looking for?" Mike asked.

"Seventeen of them, king size."

"My phone must be acting up, did you say seventies king size or did you say seventeen like the number after sixteen?"

"I said seventeen Mike, money is not a problem. Whatever the cost, I'll settle it now so you know that I'm serious. We'll be there Friday and will be staying for two weeks. If it's a problem then we can stay at the Fontainebleau, we're tied in with you so I wanted to spend my money with family first."

"No, it's no problem. I'll consolidate my current reserves to the bottom two floors and rent you the top floor. How's that sound?"

"Sounds magnificent my friend. Who's your emcee and DJ now?"

"Still Geenius on the board and DJ VLS on the mic still. I'll let them know you're coming down to stay with us for a while."

"Thanks bro, I'll see you guys Friday."

Miami was like my second home and when me or my family came to town we got the full home treatment.

Our first day we all rented a yacht each. That way everyone had their own privacy with their significant other or lady friend for the occasion.

For dinner the yachts all reversed into a circle and tethered together with a floating glass floor in the center. A plank was connected for easy access to the glass surface.

Tables and chairs were set up and we had dinner over the Atlantic Ocean. It was a sight to see the ocean was lit by the lights on the hull of the boat.

Shoota made a toast. "To G.I. Joe, the man with the plan. All of this is possible because of that big ass head of yours."

I responded, "Nah gang, this is possible because of each and every last one of you. Y'all allowed me to lead y'all into battle and we came out victorious because of y'all doing y'all part. The machine doesn't work if one piece is defective."

We all toasted. "A's up or K's up till my days up!"

After dinner we returned to shore so that we could go back to our rooms.

Tanner looked out the window facing the ocean when we were back in the room. She said, "I wish we could have had sex on the platform we had dinner on. Think of the thrill of being pleasured while danger lurks below your back. If I was riding you and I seen a shark, I would fuck you like it was my last breath."

"That's all you think about, huh? Nymphomaniac in the flesh you are," I teased.

"I think about you too from time to time."

"You better think about me all the time."

"So come make me," Tanner demanded.

We screwed each other's brains out and afterwards I held up my promise and explained to her the operation that the AAG was about to unleash.

She thought for a second and then said, "I've been thinking about leaving school and being a stay at home wife."

"You can be a stay at home wife but don't quit school, babe."

"Well I've already got business administration under my belt and I'm good with organization as well. I think I can help make sure everything is run correctly and nobody is skimming off of the top," Tanner suggested.

"And how do you suggest we do that?"

"By having everybody bring all proceeds to a weekly meeting. We know how much product is out so we'll know the profits that are expected to be brought back."

"So how would we divide up who gets what?"

"What's the number one reason most drug rings fall apart?" she didn't wait on my response and pressed on, "The cross out. Someone sees someone else is eating better than them so they back door them. I say we put everything in the pot and divide it evenly, weekly. But we only divide fifty percent, you give Knuckles his thirty percent and the other twenty percent, we put into an escrow account for expansion. That way if one product doesn't make as much as the next, that person still eats like everyone else. No big i's and no little u's."

"You learned all of that in the short time you've been in school? Damn that's a brilliant concept. My wife, Mrs. Beauty, Booty and Brains," I said, squeezing and slapping her butt.

"That's not all, I have a suggestion on the operational side as well. I don't like the idea of just anybody being able to go to the warehouse and get their product, I think we should have a delivery system. I've got a friend that works for the postal service, we can have Stuck get the orders from the guys by a certain time in the morning and Lotta, my postal friend, will deliver their product to them. Now accountability won't be an issue. We can have Stuck trail her to be sure the deliveries are made. My homegirl, Billi, is into banking, I'll have her on the books and I'll work with her on the inventory. There's no way we can lose."

"Did I ever tell you that I love you?"

"Then get down on your knees and eat your way to my heart," she demanded.

I ate her out until she cried and begged me to stop. She literally ran up the wall trying to get away from me.

DJ VLS had a VIP section set up for us later that evening. When we were seated Geenius started playing St. Louie by Nelly.

VLS announced over the mic, "St. Louis' AAG is in the building, show my people some love."

The whole crowd went wild as if they knew who we were. Then the sparkles hit the air and the bottles were on the way to our section.

I explained the order of operations to everyone before we got too drunk and asked if there were any questions.

They all agreed and said that they were wondering how the products that didn't cost as much would be able to compete with the businesses and the more expensive drugs.

Moto to live by: Eat with the same people you starve with, eat with them and don't cheat them.

We partied and bullshited the entire two weeks that we spent in Miami on South Beach.

Mike made sure we were as comfortable as possible for the entire stay.

"Getting ready to depart eh? How much time do you have before your flight leaves?" Mike came to the room and asked the day we were scheduled to check out.

"We have about six hours left, me and the Mrs. were going to enjoy some beach time before we left," I answered.

He waved me off and spoke to Tanner, "You look like the fun type, what you say I set you guys up with an experience of a lifetime? One you wouldn't want to pass up, I promise."

"What do you have in mind Mike," Tanner asked with her interest piqued.

"A few years back me and the wife were having trouble in the bedroom…"

I cut him off. "Hell no, if you even think I'll let you touch my wife, I'll throw you out of this fucking window!" I threatened.

"Calm down kid, as I was saying, Tanner. We wanted to spice things up so I hooked up with one of my pilots and started a skydiving experience for couples. You two will be tethered to the inside of a plexiglass cubicle, in the nude. The first ten thousand feet is a free fall then the parachute deploys as you settle into the ocean."

"Nope, last time I thought about jumping from a plane somebody kicked me out of it. Nope, uh-uh, not doing it." I was shaking my head.

Tanner folded her arms and pouted her lips. "Don't be a bitch, Husband. I want to do it."

Mike tagged in, "Believe me brother, you'll never have sex like this in your lifetime. Just from the adrenaline rush alone is enough to make you bust a fatty. So how about it?"

Before I could decline again Tanner interjected, "We'll be there, text us the info, Mike."

"Cool, I'll get my pilot to get the plane ready and have a car here to pick you up in an hour."

As Mike was leaving I yelled out, "That ten thousand dollar tip just got reduced to ten dollars, Bucko."

He chuckled. "Harsh, I'm sure you'll change your mind," he said as he closed the door.

An hour and forty five minutes later I was being pushed out of a plane, again. Only difference that time was that I was in a plexiglass box, stark naked.

I was so afraid of heights that I had to train my attention on something other than us falling, I buried my face into Tanner's legs.

Two licks later she was exploding like a popped water balloon. Mike wasn't lying. She mounted me and I came the first stroke.

Gravity played no favorites, position after position we were constantly climaxing.

Our falling freak shack landed fifteen minutes later in the coral reef. We asked if we could have one more round while we floated in the box. They approved of it and Tanner and I went at it like two mutts in heat.

Mike was right, not only did I change my mind after the experience, I doubled the tip.

Afraid of heights or not, that was an experience for the ages.

CHAPTER 43

I set up a meeting with Knuckles before he departed town our first day back in the city. I explained to him the suggestions that Tanner made and let him know that the guys agreed.

He looked pleased. "If you weren't already married to her I would have suggested that you do that immediately. A successful man is only as successful as his spouse."

"Roger that, Knucks. Are we all set to move forward with the op?"

"Yes, the warehouse is all stocked up, Fox and I got it all squared away. We used a fire truck that we had hollowed out behind the cab and I locked in a government contract with a private airstrip in Maryland Heights. Fox will meet the cargo plane there for the drops and bring the load to the warehouse. The back of the fire truck door folds down so that you won't have to offload any product outside in the open. Just back the truck up to the dock door and voilà! I'll give you till Friday to get Tanner's plan into place then it's full steam ahead."

"You've been really busy these last three weeks I see."

"Yes, very busy, so busy that I've even taken the initiative of securing locations for the legitimate businesses. All you have to do is email me the pseudonyms y'all will be using for them and I'll email the locations. Go get 'em soldier."

CHAPTER 44

Sunday I called an AAG meeting at the warehouse to discuss some last minute details and to come up with the business names.

I started in a playful manner, "Aye muthafuckas, y'all all fired now get the fuck out. Nah, I'm just kidding. Seriously, I need to cover a couple corners before we get going. Next Friday we will officially start business. Five AM every morning Stuck will be at your door to collect your orders for the day. He should be done by seven and back at the warehouse helping me fill orders no later than eight. I've changed up a little detail, since Stuck will have such an early start, Shoota has agreed to follow our mail person on the route with your drop offs. Which brings me to our mail lady. Lotta if you don't mind standing up," I said as an introduction, she stood up and waved so that I could continue. "If your package does not come from her, do not accept it. Call either me or Shoota immediately so we can investigate the situation. You will all be given secure phones. Those of you that have illegal businesses, your clientele will already have the contact info for that phone. They also know to have their orders in no later than midnight. For our legal side of business, while we were on vacation Knuckles took some money from the heist and secured locations for all of our businesses. Now we have to come up with the names we want them to be called. Who wants first?" I asked after feeling like I'd been long winded.

Fox went first. "I think we should dedicate the businesses to y'all AAG brand. Y'all logo is the Anaheim Angels logo so why don't we trademark the businesses? Like mine is Road Angels."

Everybody nodded their heads and started throwing out names to their business:

Reddot's strip club would be named, Dirty Angels.

Peezy's real estate company was to be Angel's Dream Realty.

Big Money's dealership was to be Speed of Angels Motors.

Lazy's security company would be called Securing Angels.

I asked Jizzle what he wanted to name the record company, he said Hyena Gang but that didn't fit so Borey came up with Always Achieving Greatness for AAG.

Banga and Gwalla would go back to Atlanta and start a smaller branch of business there. Since it was only them two that would be covering the southeast region, we thought it would be best to have them working together on making transactions. My cousin Tony, the one that dumped the trailer, would be the one to deliver their packages to them in the fire truck. The only catch would be that they had to have their weekly orders in by Saturday night so that Sunday morning Tony could get on the road and have their product delivered to them by mid-evening.

"Next week, those of you that have legit businesses, Big Money, Peezy, Jizzle, Lazy and Fox, you all will have to shop for supplies for your locations. The following Monday, your doors should be opening for business. There will be a one million dollar limit for each business. Tanner will handle those invoices and help Reddot get the club in order. Gwalla and Banga, Knuckles has a warehouse secure for y'all and your product will be available to you Friday as well. We don't have the luxury of a mail carrier in Atl so we're buying an ambulance for transportation. Y'all will be provided with EMT uniforms so that y'all will look the part," I informed them.

"What's up with the fire trucks and ambulances bro?" Sanchez asked.

"Good question, what type of vehicles do authorities pay no attention to? Other emergency vehicles. That way no one should be pulled over for suspicious activity."

"This is some 'Now You See Me, Now You Don't' type shit," Sanchez quipped.

"Just make sure you're not seen. We're only as strong as our weakest link. I know we just got back from vacay but now it's grind time. Two Sundays from now is our first business assembly, at noon we will meet at my crib for the weekly meetings. That way the banker and mail carrier can be in attendance. Are we all good?"

Everybody nodded then said in unison, "A's up or K's up till my days up!"

CHAPTER 45

Dirty Angels' grand opening was the following Saturday. We had a VIP section designated to only AAG members. That meant if the AAG wasn't in the section then nobody was in the section and you only got in there by invitation of one of us. That's why it had the A symbol on its wall.

Opening night was jammed packed, there was barely any room on the main floor. The chicken plates were flying out of the kitchen and the dollars were flying from the ceiling.

For that special occasion we booked the hottest dancers in the area and the hottest artist to perform. Lil Dirk, Key Glock and Icewear Vezzo made guest appearances, they brought the city out.

Jhu, one of the young guns of the AAG was good at entertaining so we had him and the homie Jimzel promoting the whole fiasco.

Shoota tapped me on the shoulder. "There go them cat ass niggas, gang. I'm finna act up in this muhfucka!"

I held him back. "Let me take this one, Shoota. I think I know a way to take over their business or at least eat off of them."

Tanner and Day were in the back room managing the talent so I sent Day a picture and a text: Remember what we talked about? That's your target, I'll be right behind you the whole trip.

She texted back: On it Daddy. Twenty minutes later Day was in the VIP across from us with the Lex gang. Me and Shoota left out of our section and walked over to them.

"What's up crabs I mean cats," I taunted.

"Look what the mutt shelter let out. The fuck you snoops want?" the leader asked me while the rest of his crew surrounded us.

We both were packing twin golden Desert Eagles and within a second we had all four of them out and aimed while we stood back to back.

Shoota said, "Aht-aht, I wouldn't do that if I were you."

Reece shot back, "Y'all slobs that much of some bitches that y'all paid to get y'all bangas in the club?"

I waved my gun around the club. "Take a look around you dummy, all red everything, Angels logo in the name of the place and in the main VIP. You don't get searched when you own the club. Tell yo kittens to chill before me and Shoota start a crab boil in this bitch. Now let's get down to business."

He turned furious. "I'll never do business with you mutts. Eat a dick and get the fuck outta my face."

I put my guns back in my shoulder holsters and pointed at him. "Suit yourself but I'm gonna make you eat those words, I promise."

I nodded to Day as we turned to walk off, she knew what had to be done.

An hour after the club closed, Me and Tanner pulled up to the prearranged location.

Day's job was to take Reece, the dude from the club, back to one of our display houses for Angel's Dream Realty and seduce him until we got there. I told her to bring out the freaky stuff to get him comfortable.

Tanner went in and I stood at the door. I could hear him in the living room.

"Damn, I get two for one? I might have to make you my main bitch," he said to Day.

Day responded, "My girlfriend only allows threesomes if we can handcuff the guy. She's a control freak and will get turned off if the guy gets too weird."

"Shit y'all hoes can hog tie me as long as I get to fuck both of y'all," he told her.

Tanner said, "Hog tying is so barbaric, I'm into whips and chains but we'll start slow with handcuffs and ease you along into our world, deal?"

He held out his hands for them to handcuff.

They sat him in a chair and cuffed his hands to the back legs of the chair and his legs to the front legs of it.

Day started sucking his dick as instructed and Tanner went into the kitchen. You could hear the stove ignite.

When she walked back into the living room Reece said, "When you gonna' get over here and help your girlfriend out? I got enough for both of y'all."

"Right before you cum I'll join in. Believe me, you're in for a treat." That was her way to get to him to warn her when he was close.

It only took Day twelve minutes to make buddy breathing get heavy.

"Okay bitch, I'm almost there. Get down here and help your bitch," Reece demanded.

That was my cue to walk in. We made eye contact.

He asked, "What kind of queer ass shit you got goin' on, mutt?"

That shot didn't make a difference, he was already too close and Day was going too hard. He started cumming and she bit his dick off.

Reece started screaming and thrashing in the chair like a bucking bronco.

While he was still screaming, Day stood up and put his dick in his mouth. The fucked up part is that it was still oozing sperm.

Fucking gross.

He tried to spit it out but Day held it in while Tanner duct taped it in there so he wouldn't be able to.

Throw up was oozing through the top and bottom of the tape. At least I thought it was throw up.

I got straight down to business. "Told you I was going to make you eat those words. So look, this is my business proposal for you. From this point forward, you get your supply from the AAG. Since we had to do this the hard way you keep sixty and pay us forty. Y'all will get daily deliveries and orders are to be in before midnight the day before. All that gun play is dead, deal?"

He was taking too much time to accept.

"You don't have much time, the quicker you answer, the quicker I'll have them patch and stitch you up," I offered him.

He nodded and started mumbling through the tape.

"Please whatever y'all want, y'all got it. Just don't let me bleed out," he said when Tanner snatched the tape off.

"You promise?" I asked jokingly.

"Man this ain't a good time to be playing," Reece stated.

"Oh, I'm not a mutt or a snoop or slob now huh, I guess since you're being nice. Day go ahead and close him up," I instructed.

Tanner went to the kitchen and turned the stove off. While the recent events were unfolding she had a metal candle holder sitting on the stove. She came back into the room and the candle holder was glowing because it was so hot.

Day took it and jammed it on the hole that once held the piece that defined his gender.

Reece passed out from screaming so hard or maybe it was the shock. The girls put his pants back on him and his meat in his pocket, I threw a bucket of ice water on him and he came back to consciousness.

I slapped him on his shoulder and laughed. "Remember our deal, see you later, Dickless."

I turned the recording system off and walked out the door. Lazy, Stuck and Eyes would be there soon to drop Reece off in his hood then ditch and burn his car.

I had to threaten Eyes not to kill him, we needed him to set the plan in motion.

CHAPTER 46

"Breaking news, A high ranking member of the Rolling Lex Gangsters has been found dead this morning. He was found hanging from a balcony in his North City home. At this time the authorities have ruled it as a suicide but failed to go any further in detail. This has been a KMOV news update," I heard through the TV waking me up.

"Fuck! I told that hot headed mothafucka not to kill the nigga," I yelled when a picture of Reece flashed across the screen.

Tanner looked worried. "Babe, maybe he didn't do it. They said it was ruled a suicide."

I ignored her and called Lazy. "Gang, what the fuck? I thought I told y'all to make sure Eyes didn't kill the nigga!" I yelled.

"G.I. Joe, he didn't bro, we dropped the nigga off like you asked. That was it, we went to the Goody Goody right afterwards."

"Man something ain't right, I gotta find out what the hell is going on. I'll hit you later."

My phone rang an hour later. "What's up, is this G.I. Joe?"

"Yea this G.I., who is this?" I answered.

"This Cire, Reece gave me a message to have a meeting with you."

"The fuck? Y'all niggas think y'all goin' score that easy? I ain't no rook at this shit, y'all want me y'all gotta play ball!"

"Any location, your call and it'll be just me alone," Cire negotiated.

"Alright, I'll drop a pin in about an hour, go to the Arch and I'll drop my pin. If you aren't alone and at the location in five minutes, I'm in the wind and you're dead," I promised.

I hung up and called Shoota. "Cire just called requesting a meeting. Let's get set up in the OPz and in an hour I'll meet with him."

"Alright gang, I'm about to hit Stuck and Lazy to secure a spot for us."

"Bet that."

An hour and five minutes later Cire was pulling into the meeting location. Punctuality meant everything for that moment. Eyes and Shoota were training their sights on him.

"One wrong move and you'll be a steamed crab," Shoota said to him.

Cire stepped out of the car with his hand held in the air. Eyes searched him and took the note he held in his hand.

"Reece left this for us before he hung himself," Cire told me.

The note read: I'm sorry that I have to leave y'all like this but last night something was taken from me that I can't live life without. Things were done to me that made my decision solidified. I never want any of you to endure what I have so in my departure, I want y'all to do business with the AAG mutts. They have evil within their ranks, do not cross them. I made a deal with the devil, forty percent is their cut. Meet with G.I. Joe and they'll move forward with you in my place. I'm sorry that I can't lead y'all through this but everything is going to be alright. When you meet with them make sure they know I'm writing a suicide note for my death and they have no reason to worry about the laws. C-safe my boy, I'll see y'all on the other side.

I looked up almost laughing. "This some soul touching shit. So that's what this is about, business? You should have just said that on the phone."

"I tried, you went off too fast. Whatever y'all did to bro had him extremely shook. I never heard him sound like that, all of the bass was gone from his voice. He begged us to let there be peace and go by what y'all say. You have us at your disposal."

"Let's get one thing straight, if I even think that it's some backdoor shit shaking, you'll be joining your dickless leader. And we'll be snatching all truces off of the table," I promised.

"Understood, so how do we get the product?" Cire asked right away.

"Call this number by midnight and you'll get your deliveries around three PM, daily. Y'all nickel and dime hustlers anyway so make it work until the next day."

I gave him Shoota's number since I knew they feared him, he'd keep them in line.

When Cire left Shoota asked, "You think they'll be able to survive with only one delivery and having to pay forty percent, G.I. Joe? And what happens if they sell out before three?"

"That's the point, eventually their clientele will be available for our bean patrol boys and we'll drive them out of business for good. Then the whole market will belong to us.

Classic divide and conquer, gang. AAG will be the name of the city before too long," I promised.

He side eyed me. "Man you really do have some evil shit going on in your head, that war fucked you up. I'm glad we're on the same side, it's hard to kill niggas that don't have any boundaries."

"One thing for sure, I'll never turn my back on my brothers, it's A's up or K's up till my days up!"

"No doubt about it. So what did you do to dude to make him hang it up?"

I did my best Grinch smile. "Call a meeting at my house for five o'clock and I'll show y'all."

At 5PM sharp the whole gang was in my basement theater. Tanner and Day left to go grab a big order of Mack's Chicken for the meeting before the gang arrived and would be returning shortly.

"Damn G.I. Joe, who is the fine lil' piece of meat that's with Tanner?

Put me in the game," Sanchez said when the girls came down the stairs with the food.

"That's Day, she's our personal little helper around here. She's off limits, she belongs to me and Tanner unless I send her at a nigga and after you witness what I'm about to show y'all you wouldn't want her sent your way, brodie," I said followed by a wink.

"Man y'all got some freaky ass shit going on around this joint. How the hell are you married with a live-in girlfriend? Teach me the way Sensei," a shocked Jizzle stated.

After everybody was fed the girls left and went upstairs.

I stood up. "Before I pressed play, if anybody has a squeamish stomach, feel free to leave now. Oh and parental discretion is advised," I warned before I pressed play.

Shoota shouted, "G.I., you brought us all the way out here to watch a porno? Something is wrong with you dude."

When they saw who it was in the video they all leaned closer.

Deuce said, "That's Reece and ol' girl upstairs ain't it?"

"Will y'all niggas just sit back and watch?" I instructed.

When Tanner came into view the question flew. "Don't tell me you let him fuck your wife before he killed himself," Shoota the genius asked.

As soon as he saw me come into view Sanchez said, "G.I. Joe, if you're on some fruity shit, I'll kill you right now, you won't have to worry about the Lex, I swear to God."

"Sanchez shut the fuck up, you and Shoota. Watch the damn show," I yelled.

When Day bit his joint off the whole crew started clenching their legs together tightly. Then they saw her put it in his mouth, everybody started gagging.

I was laughing. "I told him in the club I would make him eat his words."

Reddot said, "Man, you one sick dude, no wonder he hung it up. He ain't got no manhood anymore. Now imma be scared to get head from my bitch now. Thanks bruh."

"We got their business now right? And we put fear in them niggas heart, we own the Lex now," I told them.

After they watched and laughed at the video three more times they all finally left.

Something about watching my ladies in action sparked a fire in my pants. We retired to the sex room, I wanted to fuck them through the gloryhole wall.

CHAPTER 47

Thursday the gang wanted to hit Frontenac Mall, our work day was over so we all went together.

Driving down the highway in a line made me miss my CD days overseas.

Thirty minutes after being in Saks Fifth some younger Lex members walked in. As we shopped the sales people were ringing up our items, we had that much merchandise.

One of their young guns pushed up on Eyes. "Y'all niggas goin' pay for what y'all did to the big homie, that's on Lex Ave!"

I grabbed the young stepper by the back of his neck and put my Desert Eagle up under his chin.

"Didn't your dickless, I mean fearless leader teach you anything in his abrupt departure? AAG runs this fucking city, so either get down or lay down, pussy!" I threatened.

"I guess I gotta lay down, we don't fall in line with mutts," he spat back.

I turned and nodded to Shoota, he made the call to Cire.

"Yo lil' homies just fucked you. You niggas line has ran dry. Have that package ready by eight tonight, forty percent and not a penny short," Shoota instructed and ended the call.

As I was about to pistol whip the little hermit, the mall's manager came running into the store.

"What seems to be the problem, Mr.?" she asked.

"Well it seems that you can't keep your mall free of sexually transmitted diseases, you got crabs walking around here itching people that's trying to shop. And you can call me G.I. Joe."

"Well I'm the mall's manager, Niema. Nice to meet you Mr. G.I. Joe, I'll have security to escort the problem away from the premises immediately . That won't be an issue. While you guys finish up shopping the store manager has offered to close the gates until you're finished. That way we can guarantee there will be no further interruptions."

I pushed my captive prey away. "You should thank this nice lady for saving you, I was just about to crack your shell in this bitch. Next time you see one of us you better stare at the ground. And remember when y'all are selling water bottles on Natural Bridge and Kingshighway, that forty percent of y'all proceeds go to the AAG, pussy!"

Our total came up to a quarter of a million when we were all done shopping and checked out.

Niema stuck around and gave us her business card. "Whenever you gentlemen would like to shop just give me a call and we'll set up an appointment to get you as much privacy as possible. We value your business and we will accommodate your unique needs."

I shook her hand. "Thank you Niema, the way you handled that situation today was quite exquisite. We look forward to doing business with you in the future."

Sanchez caught me before I stepped into my truck. "Aye bro, I went to this new restaurant in the Central West End last night. Gang, when I tell you the food was the best I've ever tasted, I mean exactly that. The owner serves your food himself, it's real elegant like. Hit up Tanner and see if she'll meet us there. I got something hot coming through too."

"Alright go ahead, I'm following you. I'll hit her up along the way."

Tanner and Day were getting manicures and pedicures done so she couldn't make it. She told me to go ahead and go, just bring them plates back.

Something exotic was waiting on Sanchez when we pulled up to Bait, the restaurant. She had the table booked for us already so we walked right in and got seated.

I'm not the third wheel type so I took the table across from them.

Half way through my meal I felt a presence standing to the left of me. I looked up and Officer Williams was smiling down at me.

"May I have a seat?" She asked, pointing to the empty chair across from me.

"Sure, I don't see why not," I said and went back to eating and crunching numbers on my phone.

"So where's wifey? I didn't think she'd let a man like you wander too far out of her sights," she said, giving me those bedroom eyes again.

"She's doing womanly stuff so I'm all alone for the day. What can I do for you, Officer Williams? I don't take you as the chatty type, you tracked me down for a reason."

"Straight to the point I see, well let's get down to it. I'm sure you've heard about one of your rivals, Reece's recent demise…"

I stopped her. "Since when does homicide cover suicides Ms. Williams?"

"I see news gets around fast."

"When something hits Channel Four News I rarely miss it. So what are you here interrogating me for a suicide for?" I asked, showing my annoyance.

"Well I see that's the thing, some time before he hung himself, let's just say he lost his manhood..."

I stopped her again. "Ms. Williams, I fuck women only. On top of that I'm married as you know, I assure you that I've never taken any man's manhood."

"Mr. Khrist, or should I call you G.I. Joe?"

"Mr. Khrist will be fine."

"Okay Mr. Khrist, that's not the sense that I meant. Mr. Reece's penis was dismembered from his body before he quote unquote hung himself. I was wondering if you may know something since your gangs have an ongoing feud."

"Gang? Who said I'm in a gang? I showed you my military ID, I work for Uncle Sam."

"Let's cut the bullshit, alright? Do you know how I knew exactly where you'd be at this moment?"

I mugged Sanchez and said to Officer Williams, "Enlighten me."

She shook her head. "Nope, not him," she slid her foot up my leg to my crotch and continued, "Tell you what, give me what I want and I'll give you all the answers that you need."

"As I fore-mentioned, I'm married and quite frankly, I don't think my wife would be too thrilled about you attempting to seduce me. Have a good night, Officer."

She threw her business card on the table. "In case you lost the first one and little miss wifey let's you off the leash. I'll be seeing you around," she said as she got up to leave.

I stared Sanchez down. "Bro how the fuck did she know we would be here?"

"On the set bro, I don't know. The only people that knew we were coming here were the people that were with us. You saw me clutching the blizzy, I woulda put her down if she moved wrong."

"Then what? We'd be up under the jail. I gotta hit Tanner. Text the gang and let them know to keep their eyes peeled and stop operations until further notice," I demanded.

"I did that when she walked in, they're all sitting down at the Schnucks just in case."

***

"She said what?!" Tanner yelled through the phone.

"Yea babe, she said the only way she'll give me any info is if she gets what she wants. She's gotta have a source, there's no way she should know about any of the shit she just said."

"You have to go find out what she knows. I hate to say it, but you're

going to have to give it to her. That
way we can control her by letting her
think she's got the reins."

"Tanner, I'm not a piece of meat
that gets picked up when needed."

"Got dammit, you want to wake up
in prison for the rest of your life?
Make the fucking call now!" she
hung up before I could protest any
further.

Officer Williams picked up on the
first ring. "I figured you'd come to
your senses soon enough."

I could hear the pleasure in her
voice but I couldn't help but to think
how she knew who I was. That really
didn't matter though.

"When and where," was all that I
asked.

"Well I've got a lunch break here in
thirty minutes and I'm still in the
area, so let's do the Chase Plaza
Hotel."

"I didn't know cops could afford
such luxuries on y'all broke ass
salaries," I said, being rude so that
she didn't think that I needed her.

"We can't, that's why you'll be footing the tab and if you want what I've got then bring your A-game."

"All I know is the A," I said then hung up.

CHAPTER 48

We had an emergency meeting for the original members at my house after I left the Chase.

"So it's come to my attention that we've got ourselves a rat in the crew. Eyes, did you know that Pedro was picked up over the weekend by Task Force?" I asked.

"No, he hasn't said anything to me about it. Why what happened?" Eyes questioned.

"He spilled his guts is what happened, about the whole operation. Luckily we were able to catch it because they were planning to move on the warehouse Monday morning while we were filling orders. He put fucking trackers on all of our cars while we had the water balloon fight in the hood Tuesday. Stuck and Lazy swept all of them clean so that we can move around freely again."

Deuce asked, "So what, we gotta stay shut down? We just got started."

"Nah, I think we're going to promote Mr. Pedro. He wants to set somebody up then he's going to set himself up. Eyes, bring him to the warehouse in two hours. We'll have everything set up by then, text him now and tell him we want him to deliver a load to the old K-Mart on Manchester."

"What if he says it's too late?" he asked.

"Then tell him that if he completes tonight's run, Monday he'll have his own line. You gotta push him," I suggested.

"Bet that."

Pedro was sitting across from me in the warehouse office two hours later.

"So I hear you've been putting in some real work out there, I like what I hear. I need this pack taken to the Chicos on the south, do you think you can handle that?" I asked him.

"Yeah, let me call my girl and let her know I'll be home late tonight. I don't want her to be too worried," Pedro said.

"Alright, that's cool. What are you afraid to be lovey dovey with yo' hoe in front of me or something?" I asked when I saw Pedro start to get up.

"Uh, nah. I just, I just wanted to do it in private. She be wanting to kiss through the phone and shit. I can't be looking soft in front of yall. You know what I mean?"

"Yeah, I know exactly what you mean. Go handle your business, I'm sure they'll have the car packed real soon."

"Is Eyes going to be riding with me," Pedro asked when he walked back into the office.

"You need daddy to hold your hand? I thought you were a big boy now."

"I just thought that maybe he could show me how it's done since it is my first run."

This nigga must think I'm stupid.

"You'll be going alone, Eyes will be going on a hit for us tonight. I have faith in you. Go get 'em tiger. And if it makes your girl feel better, lie to her and tell her that Eyes is riding with you."

He tried to leave again but I stopped him. "No, you can make that call right here. I'm sure she got enough kisses for one night," I said sternly.

He made the call and relayed the information.

I walked him into the loading area, when we got there Relex was closing the trunk. Pedro's eyes got big when he saw all the duffle bags that were in there.

As he got into the driver seat I said to him, "Just be smooth and you'll be fine, you got this. Oh and one more thing, leave your phone. The people can track you by cell towers, we like to be discreet on these runs."

He panicked but he obeyed when I held my hand out. He looked over at the passenger seat and asked, "What's with the life size doll?"

"So they don't think that you're alone and try to rob you because you're a newbie."

"Good thing it's night time," he said, trying to laugh off his nervousness.

"Alright get out of here, we don't want to keep the clientele waiting," I said as I shit the door.

Pedro pulled into the K-Mart lot while I was on FaceTime with Reddot and Peezy. They were sitting across the street in a car lot that belonged to a buddy of mine from high school.

We had a dummy car parked in the lot where the delivery was supposed to be made. Inside the car were four life sized dolls with ski masks and Mexican attire.

Peezy hit the lock button on the key fob to the dummy car so that the lights would flash and Pedro would know where to go.

Pedro headed to that car.

The entire task force pulled up and surrounded both cars. Luckily for us the police are bigger dummies than the ones we had in the cars. They pulled so close that their front bumpers touched both cars to box them in.

They all jumped out with their guns drawn. Peezy and Reddot pressed the buttons on the detonators.

The blast was so bright that it hurt my eyes through the phone.

It was time for the grand finale.

Eyes threw together a quick team of hitters; Fatt Rell, Borey, Animal, Foeside and Big Money. When the blast went off they came from behind the building and made sure everyone was dead. Those who weren't were executed.

GAME OVER

Officer Williams called my SAT phone. "Nice move, the whole task force is KIA. Every officer in the city is on their way out to the scene. I cleaned up the task force office so anything leading to their operation on the AAG has been destroyed. Now don't forget to hold up the rest of the deal."

"I won't, I'm personally enroute to handle it myself," I told her.

"I knew I could count on you. I'll see you around."

CHAPTER 49

"Breaking news , Chief of Police Roderick White was the victim of a car bombing that happened this morning. This bombing came a couple hours after a drug task force was completely taken out by a separate bombing overnight. Captain Li Williams has been named the interim Chief of Police. We'll send it over to our ground crew. Chief Williams is expected to make an appearance at a press conference," the news anchor said on tv.

The screen switched to Chief Williams taking the podium on the stage.

"I want to thank you all for being here today. Unfortunately it is under these conditions. The St. Louis City police would like to extend our condolences to the families of the twenty seven officers that were killed in action in the early morning hours. The attacks have been claimed as a terrorist attack by a group of Middle Eastern insurgents who call themselves Alfi-Allahabad. We are working closely with Washington to get to the bottom of this situation. That's all of the information that we have at the moment," she finished and exited the stage without taking any questions.

"That bitch is a good ass actor," I said.

"Tanner looked at me and said, "Too good, you know we're going to have to kill her right?"

"That's what I was afraid of."

CHAPTER 50

Sunday rolled around and we were having our first meeting.

"First things first, these last two weeks have been hell. Throughout all of the obstacles we've had to bulldoze or hurdle, we made it. I believed we took care of all problems and from here on out it should be smooth sailing," Shoota said, allowing me to have a break.

I introduced Billi to the crew. She took over from there. "This week's gross is seven point three million. One point forty six will go into the escrow for business, two point two goes to Mr. Moose and everyone's cut for the week is two hundred fifteen thousand, seven hundred and five dollars. G.I. Joe has left it up to you to pay your employees their share. That's all I have for the week, are there any questions that you all have for me?"

Sanchez raised his hands. "Yeah, when can I clap them cheeks?"

"How about never. Now are there any questions about business?" she shot back.

Animal asked. "Yeah, how come Knuckles cut is so big and ours is so small?"

I took the question. "Because he put this operation together, he provides the clientele, the plane for the cargo, the airstrip for the plane, the product itself and our protection from the government forces. You want a larger paycheck, we gotta pull in more business on the legal side and more clientele on the illegal side. There's a lot of us and we split everything evenly so no one has more than the next."

He laughed. "Shit, show me where the product is and I'll walk and get it myself for two point two million dollars."

"Unless you magically turn into Moses, I doubt you'll be walking to get this cargo."

Everybody laughed at Animal.

When everyone left I sat on the couch and turned on some football, my Ravens were dominating the Steelers.

Tanner came and sat on my lap. "I love the way you handle business. Most people in your position would be trying to have all the power and all the money. You're so down to Earth and humble when it comes to business."

"Knuckles told me that one is only as successful as their spouse, so I'm this way because of you."

She kissed me then said, "Knuckles is a smart man."

"Yeah I know, besides, I'd rather eat with the team than compete with them. There's enough revenue to go around., no sense in being greedy. You taught me that greed be niggas downfall."

"Now you're the smart man. I love you, Husband."

"I love you more, Wife."

"Day is running some errands for me, she'll be gone for a while. How about you sit back and relax, watch your game and let me please you for a change."

"You always please me babe."

"I mean without the return. You always eat my pussy until I fall asleep or if you don't have the energy to fuck me. So let me just return the favor."

"That's going to be hard for me to do, boo. You know that'll make me crave you," I warned.

"Then fight it. Pay attention to your team and let me do my job," she said while rubbing her finger around my crotch.

Tanner slid down to her knees and sucked me until I was running up the couch while I watched the Ravens run away with the game.

CHAPTER 51

Six months had passed and it was the first warm day in March. Business was booming, everybody's weekly cut was up to a million per week. The legit companies were now seeing constant consumers. The record label had both artists on tour and their singles were spinning everywhere. Luh Borey had a single featuring Luh Iraq titled Grind.m, Fatt Rell's single was called Shots Fired featuring K-Twice. Both singles were getting positive feedback and kept those boys busy. Jiizzle was on the lookout for more talent that was coming out of the city.

Big Money's dealership had cars flying through the gates almost as soon as they touched the lots. Most of the business came from the local drug dealers because they knew who was behind the dealership and they wouldn't be questioned bringing cash.

Peezy was flipping houses like he was SpongeBob at the Krusty Krab.

Reddot's Dirty Angels became a popular spot for the night scene. After Sada Baby flooded the stage with Ben Franks all the notable dancers were fighting to be house regulars.

Business was great.

I pulled up to Pop's house on Ashland. When I parked and got out a patrol car was driving past, they hit a U-turn and hit the emergency lights.

The patrolman and his partner jumped out of the car. "Well, well, well, if it isn't young Escobar. I see your dreams finally came true," the driver said, pointing to the G-Wagon.

"It's been a long time Mr. Billy Club. I'm guessing your partner is Billy Club Jr. To answer your question, no my dreams haven't come true because my grandfather let you live," I shot back.

He broke out laughing. "Billy Club, that's funny, I have a new name now, it's Glock Nineteen. All I have to do is say I feared for my life and nobody will ask any questions while your black ass rots in a grave."

"Woah, is that the way to treat military personnel, with disrespect or is it just my good looks that gets me this treatment?"

"I didn't know Uncle Sam allowed thugs into his ranks, they must be really desperate these days."

"Not as desperate as SLMPD, to let a bunch of incestuous Hills Have Eyes peckerwoods like yourself into its ranks. But hey, who's keeping score?" I laughed that time.

My face was pressed so hard up against my truck that I felt it turning hot.

Billy Club Jr. started ransacking the interior of the truck.

I yelled out, "Careful, I wouldn't want to have to take from your daughter slash sister's college fund to replace anything in there."

That got my face pressed harder into the hood. I laughed even harder.

Billy Club Jr. held up a small baggie of heroin when he came out of the truck from his search.

He pointed at me. "Gotcha cuz."

"I'm not a cuz or your cuz, my family doesn't hump each other. And you should say no to drugs, you might not grow up big and strong like your Papa here," I shot back.

"That's okay, you'll have all the time to crack all the jokes you want while you're down at central booking."

"You must be joking, you know damn well that shit ain't mine," I said angrily. My smile was gone.

He rubbed the baggie on my face. "DNA says otherwise."

When I got to booking I asked the fingerprint tech to have Chief Williams to come see me.

Forty five minutes later Williams walked in with her Chief uniform on all high and mighty. She excused the officer that was attending the holding cells.

"What the hell are you doing here?" she asked after stepping to my cell.

"Two of your officers planted some dope on me," I responded with a hard tone.

She started laughing. "It won't stick if they freecased you."

"Yeah, that's what I said then he rubbed the plastic on my face."

That wiped her smile away too. "Don't worry, I'll handle it." She looked me up and down. "You know this has always been a fantasy of mine."

"What to see me locked up?"

"No, to get fucked through the lockup bars. Put your hands through the gate," she demanded.

Li handcuffed my hands together so that there was a bar separating my arms. She started rubbing my dick through my jogging pants. When it was rock solid she pulled it out and through the bars then she knelt down.

Right when she was about to close her mouth around it I snatched my dick back away from her.

"Under one condition," I told her.

She looked up at me with puppy eyes. "All you have to do is name it."

"The two that freecased me must be fired from the force immediately," I demanded.

She grabbed my hard-on and yanked it back to her. "Consider it done."

Williams sucked me off until she came then she stood up and turned around. She pulled up her shirt and stuck me in her.

We fucked for a good twenty minutes, when she felt my dick pulsating inside of her, she went down to her knees and started the twist and pull with one hand and the other massaging my sack. "Cum on my face," she begged.

The way I painted her face I think I may start calling myself Picasso.

Billy Club Sr. and Jr. were getting out of their squad car when I was walking out of the station.

I pointed two trigger fingers at them. "Gotcha cuz. If y'all ever need employment look me up, my toilet attendant just quit this morning."

Stuck was sitting on the hood of his car laughing. We got in the car and headed back to the zone.

There's always another obstacle when you clear one.

Shoota was the first to the car as we pulled up. "Bro, where have you been? We've been calling you for an hour."

"I was down at central booking, two pigs tried to freecase me. Chief Williams fired both of them though. What's up though gang, why is everybody looking all troubled and gloomy?" I asked.

"Gwalla just called, Banga got shot and killed a few hours ago," Shoota said with tears in his eyes.

"What?! How the fuck did that happen?"

"I don't know, gang. I already set up thirty with Billi to take care of his funeral."

"Alright, Knuckles is from down that way, I'll give him a call and see what he can come up with. Make sure Gwalla finds out what happened."

I hit Knuckles on the SAT phone.

"Khrist, what's up golden boy? I see business is going pretty swell under your command. What can I do for you?" Knuckles asked.

"You remember the bro Banga, one of my guys that takes care of things in the southeast region for us?"

"Yep, what's up with him? He hasn't gone rogue has he?"

"No not at all, he was killed down there a few hours ago. I was wondering if you could put your ears to the streets for me?"

"Yeah, that's no biggie. I have a couple nephews up that way that run the streets, I'll get on the horn with them."

Shoota grabbed my attention. "Gwalla said Banga went to make a play on his own because he couldn't get in touch with him. He said it happened on Six Flags Drive."

I relayed the information. "Listen Knucks, it happened on a street called Six Flags Drive down there. I'm sure the funeral is going to be down there in probably a week, I'll need some wheels and tools. Me and the guys will be flying in and we want to handle it ourselves," I told him.

"I got you, let me know when you'll be landing and I'll get my nephs to collect you from the airport."

I hung up, I needed to get home. I dapped up all the bros and got straight on the phone with the wife.

Tanner was at the warehouse with Billi finishing up some inventory so she made it home thirty minutes after I did.

I explained the whole freecase situation to her, I even told her about letting Chief Williams fuck me to get the charges dropped and the daddy brother combo fired. Then the tears took over my eyes as I told her about Banga's death.

She made me lay my head on her chest and held it while I cried. "I'm not mad at you for making that decision at the precinct, that was probably the best decision for business. I'm starting to think we should keep Williams around, she's turning out to be quite an asset to our cause. As far as Banga, I'm sure Knuckles will come through, he normally does. You and Shoota gotta stay strong to get the rest of the crew through this. I know it's hard and it hurts me to see you like this but you gotta pull it together. Let the rest of your tears fall right now then pick your head up and go take care of business like only you know how to do."

I was all out of tears when I lifted my head out of Tanner's chest. My game face was on and I was ready to go into battle with my unit.

CHAPTER 52

When we landed in Atlanta Knuckles had arranged for a shuttle service to pick us up. Four Mercedes limo vans shuttled us to the Aloft hotel downtown.

We got checked into our rooms and an hour later we met Knuckles' nephews in the conference room of the hotel. They introduced themselves as Drive and Forty/Glock.

"Why do they call you Forty?" I asked him.

"Y'all niggas talk proper as hell," he raised up his shirt and showed his Glock and pressed on, "it's Fawty."

"Alright Fawty, so why do they call you Drive or am I saying that too proper too?" I laughed.

He tossed up some keys. "Anything with fo' wheels, I can get you out that jam."

"Bet that, so y'all uncle told me that y'all found out what happened to my potna."

Fawty said, "How much is it worth to y'all?"

I saw the gang get testy. I had to get the situation under control fast.

"Thirty cash, all blue faces," I said.

"Now we talkin' Unk told us to give y'all these two suitcases." He put them on the table and opened them.

Inside were two M4s, eight MP5s and keys.

Drive gave us the information we needed and they headed out to set up for the night.

Banga's funeral was two days away and we wanted the person responsible dead before his service. It was time to get our lick back.

Soon as night fell we jumped in the three SRT-8 Jeeps that Drive provided us and went to our target's house.

I was dressed in a business suit when I rang the doorbell.

"Who isn't it?" came a woman's voice from behind the door.

It was time to put those drama classes from high school to the test. "Ma'am I'm a representative from the Atlanta Gas Company, there have been various reports of vapor seeping through the inside meters. I'm going house to house to scan for any leaks so that we can get a tech out to fix any problems before an explosion occurs."

The lock was unsecured and the lady peeled through the cracked door.

I kicked the door right into her face before she could get any words out. Guns were drawn as we ran into the house, we brought the only other occupant into the living room too.

"You look a little too old to be calling yourself Huncho," I said to the old man. I turned to the bloody faced lady. "I'm guessing you're his mother, where is he?"

"I haven't seen him in a week and a half," she said between sobs.

I turned to Eyes and Stuck. "Tie the old man up from the ceiling and tie the lady to a chair."

Once they were secured I stood in front of the lady. "So here's how this goes, you're going to FaceTime your son and get him here as soon as physically possible. Until he gets here I'm going to break a limb on the old man here every five minutes," I said pointing my thumb over my shoulder.

She was bawling hysterically but she was a tough old hag. "I will not call my only son into an ambush. Go ahead kill us and you still won't get your hands on my son," she said as she spat blood in my face.

Oh goody, it was time to get creative. I went into the kitchen and grabbed a dish towel, duct tape, a sharp knife and a pair of pliers.

I asked Shoota to hold the lady's head so she couldn't look away when I stepped back into the living room.

I opened my briefcase and pulled out a tube of super glue and a syringe. I super glued the mom's eyelids open.

The dish towel went into dad's mouth and that was duct taped there so he couldn't spit it out, he was about to get noisy.

I looked back at Mama Super Glue and said, "Last chance."

She declined again.

Cool. I cut an incision in the man's neck area, the cut went the length of his shoulders.

He was squirming so hard that Eyes and Stuck had to hold him still.

I gripped a piece of his skin and started separating his flesh from his muscles.

About five inches in Mama Super Glue gave in, "Okay, okay, please just stop. Please, I'll make the call."

Huncho picked up on the third ring. "What's up, Ma Dukes?"

I uncovered the camera and all he saw was my face covered by a red ski mask.

"Huncho, I heard you've been busy a few days ago over on Six Flags Drive," I said.

"If you touch my mama, I'll kill you," he said, shaking from being angry.

"You're a little too late," I showed him his mama's bloody face and continued, "luckily for you and Ma Dukes here, we don't kill kids or women. Now as far as dad or mom's boyfriend, he's not going to be so lucky."

I put the camera on the man.

"If you're not here alone in twenty minutes, I'll peel the rest of his skin off and every time he thinks about passing out, I'll give him a shot of adrenaline. You got twenty minutes and if you call the police, I guaran-damn-tee you I will go against my morals and I'm killing this bitch of a mother of yours!"

I peeled another inch of the man's skin so he could see that I wasn't fucking around then I hung up.

We untied the parents and
ushered them out the back door and
into a Sprinter van that Drive had
waiting.

Stuck and Eyes trailed them to the
spot that we would be
rendezvousing next.

Shoota and I went back into the
house and into the living room to
wait and watch the street.

Fifteen minutes later a black
Hellcat Charger came roaring up the
street. The tires were screeching as
it came to a stop in front of the
house. All four doors opened and
four dudes jumped out, guns in hand
and sprinted to the porch.

Show time.

Big Money, Gwalla, Sanchez and
Foeside came from the side of the
house across the street and had
their guns in the back of the head of
the two guys that brought up the
rear.

Shoota and I swung the door open
and stuck the M4s in the front two
faces.

Shoota yelled, "Step in slowly with your hands up."

The element of surprise never failed.

They all obeyed our orders. Once everybody was inside we pushed them up against the wall and searched them.
We disarmed them of their weapons.

I took Huncho's pistol and stuck it in the back of his neck. "I thought I told you to come alone, bitch. You think you're running the show here?"

"They were already with me, you said twenty minutes, I didn't have time to drop them off man. Where the fuck are my parents?" He was sweating profusely.

"Whoa, language buddy. But don't worry, we'll be joining them soon. There's one small problem, we kind of only have room for one passenger, if you catch my drift."

"Man, they don't have anything to do with this, you can leave them here and take me," Huncho begged.

"Oh, I intend to leave them here. I'll make sure they stay put." I turned to Shoota and said, "I'm gonna go grab another knife, you grab that one off of the table. I'll be right back."

The captives were shaking like a bunch of two dollar strippers when I came back into the living room.

"Y'all niggas should try to get jobs at Magic City the way y'all shivering and shaking," Sanchez said.

Huncho started begging again, "Bro please let them live, they're innocent. I swear to it, whatever it was I did it alone."

"Alright, if you insist. We'll let them live but they gotta lay down on their stomachs and hands behind their backs until we get out of the door," I promised.

The dummies did it, I had to hold myself back from laughing.

Big Money kept his MP5 on Huncho. Gwalla, Sanchez and Foeside held down the other three as me and Shoota cut the Achilles tendons on their legs. I said I'll leave them alive, I didn't say anything about being unharmed.

We all walked Huncho out to the back door to the two Jeeps that we had waiting.

We pulled up to Lake Lanier, to the spot that Fawty and Drive set up to rendezvous, an hour later.

A good ol' family reunion.

Mama Super Glue started crying when we pulled her son out of the trunk.

I pushed him down in front of his parents. "Go ahead, explain to your parents why they gotta watch you die."

"How am I supposed to explain something that I don't know," he said sternly, attempting to be tough in front of his mama.

I stuck his pistol in his eye. "Does Six Flags Drive ring any bells? I know you heard me earlier on FaceTime. Keep playing with my intelligence and I'll show you how dumb us STL boys get. Yo mama will be floating to the bottom of the lake with her hands tied to her feet."

"I swear I don't know what y'all talking about," he said with alligator tears.

"You know you can't get into heaven if the last thing you do alive is lie, right? But that's okay, we'll get you in there. You'll tell the truth soon enough," I promised.

I took the pliers out of my pocket and pulled his dad's skin further down. He started going into shock and earned himself an adrenaline boost.

Huncho started to come to his senses. "He tried to rob me, bro, he tried to rob me," he cried.

Shoota looked at him confused. "Please help me understand why someone who makes a million dollars a week would need to rob anyone. That makes sense to you G.I.? How about you Fawty?"

We both shook our heads.

I went back to peeling dad's skin off his body, I was down to his pectoral muscles.

"Alright man, I needed to come up with some money fast and jackin' was the only way I knew to get it quick. I'm sorry, man I'm sorry please let my folks go," Huncho pleaded.

Eyes shot the dad in the face point blank and he fell into the lake.

Huncho and Mama Super Glue screamed.

Shoota shot Huncho in both knees and elbows. "Now you're going to feel the pain that we feel, pussy." He took the pliers and yanked out his twelve front teeth.

Mama Super Glue passed out from fear, her eyes were still stuck open.

We tortured Huncho for twenty minutes straight. Eyes and Stuck threw him into the lake barely hanging on to his life, he'll drown eventually. Fuck 'em.

We left Mama Super Glue unharmed, women and kids were off limits. She couldn't tell too much anyway unless she could see through our ski masks. My face was the only one she saw and I wasn't from there. She'll probably starve to death out here anyway, it's a long way back to Atlanta on foot.

CHAPTER 53

Before we left Atlanta we talked Gwalla into coming back to St. Louis with us. Banga was in the ground and we got our lick back.

I called Knuckles to meet me at the hotel to discuss some business before our departure from his A to head back to our A.

"Knucks, I want to thank you for helping us find the person responsible for Banga's death. Gwalla is going back to the Lou with us so that we can all look after each other, this is a situation we don't want to experience again. In showing my gratitude to your nephews, I want to leave the business here under their command. With your blessing of course," I said as we stood in at the bar.

"I think that would be a good move. I'll supervise their movements, it's been boring sitting on my ass anyway. It'll feel good getting back in the old saddle again."

We shook on it and the AAG
headed to the airport. Business in
Atlanta was handled.

CHAPTER 54

"What's up Billi, you got some time to talk for a minute?" I asked as I walked into her office.

"Yes, what do you have for me?"

"Due to some recent events, I've been thinking about doing some land developments down on Ashland. I was trying to see how much I could borrow against the businesses for a project I have in mind?"

She clicked a few times on her mouse and hit a few keys. "With the current revenue rate that the businesses are pulling in quarterly, I could get you in the one point eight billion range. What kind of project do you have in mind?" she asked, concerned.

"I'll let you know soon enough, I have to holler at Peezy and see what he thinks."

I got up and left so that she couldn't question me anymore.

Peezy met me in the hood with a developer to give us an estimate on the build. We worked it out so that the process would stay between Peezy and myself until the project was done.

"So walk me through exactly what you're looking to get done here. Then we can talk numbers," the developer demanded.

"Have you ever seen the old movies where a town was enclosed inside of a wall? Like the medieval era?" Peezy asked him.

"If you tell me that you want to build a wall around the entire city, I'm going to lose my shit," the developer said doubtfully.

"Actually we were thinking smaller, more like a compound. It'll start at Elmbank and Newstead and end at Taylor and Natural Bridge, everything in between we want to wall in. The current houses we want demolished and replaced with thirty mini-mansions. They will all surround a forty four story building that is capable of housing condos suited for five adults," I said.

"And for this fairytale, how do you plan on getting behind the wall from the real world?" the developer shot at me.

"Underground parking. We want the garage to expand the entire premises, that's only accessible by fingerprint. We should be able to gain access to our residences from below. The condos can only be accessed by the occupant by key card. I don't care about how many men or companies it takes, you've got a year deadline!"

That brought tears of mockery to his eyes. "A year, ha, impossible."

I shook my head at Peezy. "Come on, he's not our guy."

As I turned to leave, the developer caught my arm. "Give me a year and a half and I'll get it done. But first before we talk numbers, I need you to know, the average time to let land settle is a year. I'll do it in half a year since you're adamant, it's going to take special treatment to make sure that the ground is stable. Now let's run some numbers. Thirty mini mansions at three million a piece that's ninety alone, the underground parking would tack on another ten mill, so we're already up to a hundred. Add another two fifty to that for the high rise, you're at three hundred fifty now. And let's just ballpark the wall at another ten million, that's three hundred and sixty million for reconstruction alone. The demolition will be roughly twenty million plus let's say another forty for the manpower to get the job done in your time frame," he said fastly running out of breath.

"So let's just say five hundred mill to be on the safe side. How soon can you get started? While the demo is being done y'all can work on the architectural blueprints."

"It'll take at least a month for prep and permits but your biggest hurdle will be to get the alderman and mayor to sign off on the build," the developer informed us.

"The alderman is family so that won't be a problem, I'll handle the mayor. Do what you have to do to get the ball rolling. You'll have your go ahead by next week."

We shook hands and exchanged contact information.

CHAPTER 55

Cousin Sam, the alderman of our ward, set up a meeting for me with the mayor and his wife at Kemoll's. I had a little over twenty four hours to prepare.

"Tan, where are you, hun?" I called out as I entered the house.

"In the kitchen, love," she answered.

"Does anybody around this house wear any clothes?" I asked when I walked in the kitchen and saw her cooking in the nude.

She shook her butt and said, "What's the matter, can't keep your eyes off for too long?"

"If I didn't know any better, I'd think y'all like torturing me. Go get dressed, we have to go shopping."

"Shopping for what? And the mall is about to close anyway."

"Babe just go get dressed will you? I have a couple calls that I need to make."

"But I'm cooking, Husband," she said in a whiny voice followed by a pout.

"Throw it away, we'll grab something while we're out. Go get dressed Tanner or I'm leaving without you," I threatened.

She took off running to her dressing room. She knew that me leaving without her wasn't an empty threat, I've done it numerous times before.

"Good evening, this is Niema speaking. How may I help you?" the manager from Frontenac asked when she answered the phone.

"Hey Niema, how are you? This is G.I. Joe, you gave me your number a few months back and told me if I needed to shop to give you a call."

"Oh yes, I remember you. I'm fine thanks for asking. When do you need to come in?"

"I know it's last minute and you guys are about to close up but I need to come tonight. My wife and I have dinner with the mayor tomorrow and we have to look the part," I said apologetically.

"Um, I'm not sure if I could keep the whole mall open on such a short notice, I tell you what, give me two stores that you want to shop in and I'll make it happen."

"I'm sure we can find clothes and shoes in Saks and what about Kay's?" I asked.

"Okay, just give me a call when you pull up and I'll have security escort you into the building."

"Oh gosh thank you, you're a lifesaver, Niema," I said then hung up.

"I told you we wouldn't make it by the time they closed. You made me throw my food away for nothing," Tanner yelled at me and folded her arms as we pulled up to the mall. I ignored her jab and hit dial on the last number that I called so the call went through the truck's hands free system.

"Good evening, this is Niema. How may I help you?"

"Niema, it's G.I. Joe, I'm at the front entrance," I said looking at Tanner.

"Okay, I'll be down shortly."

Niema came and let us in herself. I introduced her to Tanner, they exchanged pleasantries and she led us to Saks.

"Tan, why can't we start at Kay's? I'm sure it'll be faster," I asked.

She and Niema both laughed.

"Men know nothing about fashion," she said to Niema.

"You pick your jewelry according to your clothes, not the other way around, Husband," Tanner told me while rolling her eyes.

"Well I'm sorry madame, Versace, I didn't mean to offend you," I said in my best English butler impersonation.

Niema laughed and said, "I would have never taken you as a man that bows down to their woman after our first encounter."

That piqued Tanner's interest. "What first encounter would that be Mr. Khrist and why didn't I know about it?"

"I had to rough up one of them little cats from the Lex one day we were shopping and it must've slipped my mind after the event at Bait. My mind wasn't there, it was on the more important situation. That shit was minor."

"Uh huh, I don't like having to find out incidents in this manner. Understood?" she asked angrily.

No problem, I knew how to fix that. "Yes ma'am."

Men are straight to the point when it comes to shopping for events, women or the other hand, not so much.

My outfit was a nice fitted black Tom Ford suit with a red accent. I grabbed a pair of red suede Gucci loafers to top it off with no socks. I picked out a peach body contour dress for Tanner, she set it off with a pair of nude colored Christian Louboutin red bottoms. Those were our outfits for the dinner.

Two hours later Tanner was just finishing up her casual shopping.

It was almost midnight by the time we got to Kay's. When we entered, Tanner started acting like a kid in a candy store immediately.

"Husband, how am I supposed to pick out jewelry if I don't know the occasion?" Tanner asked in her spoiled voice.

"Can't you just match it with your outfit?"

Niema was obviously playing wingman for the night. "You have different jewelry for different occasions, if it's dinner then you can be more casual but if it's formal then you want your jewelry to pop," she said as she winked at Tanner like I wasn't standing right there watching them.

Tanner slapped her hand. "Thanks girlfriend, men are so clueless."

"Fine, we're having dinner with the mayor and his wife tomorrow evening to discuss a developmental matter. That's good enough for you, Princess?"

Thanks Niema for ruining my surprise.

She tapped her chin. "Sounds important but first we need to find you an elegant watch to go with your suit."

Seventy thousand dollars later we were finally walking out of Kay's.

When we got on the highway Tanner kicked off her shoes and put her feet on the dashboard. She started rubbing her clit through her biker shorts.

"So you're just going to ruin my seat, huh?" I asked her.

"Shhhh," she moaned.

Tanner slid her shorts off and soaked her hand with her juices then she slid her hand down my Born2Win track pants and rubbed her moisture up and down my cock.

When I was stiff she told me to lift up and she slid my bottoms down to my knees.

Road head, YES!

However, that wasn't the case.

Tanner climbed across the console and slid down on my joint. She leaned to the side so that I could still pay attention to the road then she started sucking on my neck.

"Bae, you want me to pull over? You're going to make me crash the G-Wagon."

"Please don't, the thrill of danger is making me even hornier," she moaned.

"Oh yeah? What's gotten into you?" I asked, trying to stay concentrated on the highway.

"This dick is in me baby."

"Besides that, this is new."

"That whole situation back there at the mall, you had them people open up their doors just so I could shop. My pussy was soaking the entire time, if I could've, I would have fucked you in the middle of the mall but I don't think it would have been as exciting as this," she said as she bounced up and down on me.

She rode me all the way to the house, literally then we finished having sex standing outside of my truck, in the driveway.

We went straight to the sex room when we got in the house. I got naked and laid face down on the milking table.

Tanner gave me an upper body massage while Day sat under the table and sucked on me through the hole.

I'm not even sure if I came or not, the massage knocked me out. When I woke up the wall was open and my babies were laying in the bed sleeping naked and cuddled up.

At that moment I realized that I had forgotten to stop and get Tanner something to eat. I walked in the room and woke her up to a full course meal of meat in her mouth.

CHAPTER 56

"Hello, how are you today? I would like to book your establishment tonight from the hours of eight PM until ten PM," I said into the phone to the manager of Kemoll's.

"Okay, how many guests will be dining with us tonight?"

"Just four."

"And can I get your name for the reservation?"

"Khrist, with a K."

"Thank you, I have you down as arriving at eight. If there's a line you can check in through our website."

"Excuse me ma'am, by booking the establishment, I meant the entire space."

"Well sir, I don't think that would be possible. Even if it were, the price would certainly be steep," the manager said matter of factly.

I looked at the phone, the disrespect. "How much would be steep, ma'am?"

"I would say forty to fifty thousand."

"Ok that's fine, I can pay it over the phone. Let me know when you're ready for my card number."

"Sir, I said it wouldn't be possible," she said, getting angry.

"Okay, well can I get your name and corporate's number? So I can let them know who turned down fifty thousand dollars and a visit from the mayor of the city."

I assumed that she was calling my bluff because she gave me the number and her name was Karen.

***

At 7:45 Tanner and I were getting into the elevator of a downtown high rise from their underground parking lot. Atop of that high rise was the restaurant Kemoll's.

The elevator was mirrored with a golden finish and I couldn't help but to stare at my wife through it.

"What are you looking at ugly?" Tanner asked me.

"My fine ass wife. You're wearing the shit out of that dress. That muhfucka is putting extra emphasis on those curves tonight. Then that neck piece is sitting perfectly at the peak of those titties," I teased her then but my bottom lip.

"My stylist really put me together tonight. You like what you see, Zaddy?" Tanner asked as she started gyrating on me.

"No, I love what I see. This reflection of us in the wall is perfect," I told her with a kiss on the forehead as the elevator opened.

The maitre d' greeted us. "Good evening ma'am, sir, but we're closed for the evening. If you would like, I can get you a reservation for another night," he said politely.

"No thank you, the one we have for tonight is just fine," I said gracefully.

He looked down at his computer and back up at me. "Would you happen to be Mr. Khrist, sir?"

I spread my arms. "Tada, that would be me."

"My apologies sir, you and your Mrs. can follow me and I'll get you seated."

He led us into the restaurant then to our table. "Your server will be with you momentarily while you wait on our guest of honor."

I looked at him like he had a fresh piece of bird turd stuck to his face. "I'm not important enough to be the guest of honor? Is that what you're saying? I'm almost certain that my name is on the reservations and receipt."

He turned red from embarrassment. "That's not what I meant, I'm sorry sir."

"Damn now I'm a sorry sir. Sheesh the shit storm this place has put me through today," I said, exhausted with the situation.

"No sir, that's not... I'll grab your server for you. Enjoy your evening." He ran off almost in tears.

Our server approached the table. "How are you guys doing tonight? My name is Karen, can I get you anything to drink while we wait for the arrival of the mayor?"

"There sure are a lot of you working here with the name Karen," I said while looking over the drink menu.

"No sir, I would be the same Karen that you spoke with this morning."

"Oh, that Karen, the one that told me this wasn't possible," I looked around the restaurant and continued, "Also, that fifty thousand dollars price tag that you told me, was a joke. Try ten but since their wonderful manager told me fifty, I made an extra forty thousand dollar donation. I'm sure you'll get a raise soon. My wife would like a bottle of Dom Perignon and I'll have some water please. Now run along, peasant," I said, shooing her off.

Tanner looked at me with disgust. "Why are you being so rude to these people?"

I explained to her about the phone call with Karen that morning and having to call corporate to get the dinner set up.

"Just because she was being an asshole doesn't mean you have to be one too. Kill her with kindness."

"You're right my love. You see that's why I wouldn't be able to stay afloat without you, my lifesaver."

She stared at me. "Corny bro."

The mayor and his wife walked in before I could go into to my incest speech with Tanner.

I stood up to greet them. "Mayor Bierey, thank you for accepting my invitation tonight. This is my lovely wife Tanner."

He shook her hand. "Nice to meet you madame, this is my wife Gabby."

I kissed the back of her liver spotted hand. "Nice to meet you, Mrs. Bierey."

She waved me off. "Gabby is just fine."

Time to bring out the drama class again. "Ma'am if you don't mind, I was raised in a household that taught formalities. I've lived my entire life by those teachings, yes ma'am, no sir. My grandfather would kill me if he knew I was calling someone of such importance by their first name."

"We wouldn't want to make grandfather ma now, I'll allow Mrs. Bierey on his behalf."

I bowed. "Thank you ma'am. Tanner ordered a bottle of Dom Perignon, it should be here shortly. Mr. Mayor, I didn't know your drink of choice so I didn't order you anything, my apologies."

"Don't mention it, but for future references, scotch is a gentleman's drink. You can never go wrong with that."

When Karen brought the bottle for the women and my water she took the mayor's drink order and handed us the dining menus to look over.

"So how did you come to pull this off?" he asked and swept his hand around the restaurant.

"Seems when you tell someone that the mayor will be attending their establishment, they'll move mountains to ensure your cameo is received."

I left out the part about the donation, I needed his ego through the roof on that one.

"You sure know your stuff, where did you go to school?"

"I'm a Lafayette High School of Rockwood School District alumni." I answered.

"No college?" he asked, showing his disappointment.

"No sir, I went straight into the Army after graduating high school. Did a tour in the theater and now I'm back."

"So you're done with the service now? You seem kind of young," Mr Bierey challenged.

"Negative sir, I'm still in the service. I run a special unit of my own now, I'm in the private sector if you will. I have a little freedom now."

"Sounds interesting, what type of work does your unit do?" he asked, fishing.

"I'm afraid that you don't have the security clearances to be privy to those details, sir."

"Oh, so you're a DOD guy?"

"In a way, you can say that."

Karen came and took our orders then brought out two more bottles of Dom Perignon. The wives were in their own little conversation and running through glasses of champagne.

The mayor and I chatted about my tour overseas and the jewelry that the women were wearing while we waited on our dinner to arrive.

Tanner and I had the glazed lamb chops with shrimp and garlic mashed potatoes. The Biereys had steak, rare. I don't even know what else they had, I couldn't make it past the fact that they might be real life vampires.

We didn't talk much while we ate, proper table etiquette. Afterwards, I jumped into the business while the ladies had at their drinks.

"Sir, I told you about the neighborhood that I was raised in. I've already gotten the okay from the ward's alderman, but I would like to do a land development project for the area. I want to bring back the value and quality of the inner city," I finished by walking him through the plans that I wanted to unroll.

He was all ears, then he said, "You sound like you have a great plan that you've put a lot of thought into. However, we don't back gangsters and allow them to fortify anywhere they feel the need to. How would that look for the city?"

Strike out!

"Gangsters? Sir, why would you think that I'm a gangster?" I was baffled.

"You think I come to meetings with people that I know nothing about? Before I accepted I had a full background check on you, I'm not sure what you're into but I do know that the military is backing you. Everything I asked you, I already know, I just wanted to see if you'd be truthful."

"Sir, you think the military would put a quote unquote gangster in command of one of their top secret operations?"

"Come on, cut the bullshit. Everybody knows that there are gangs in those ranks..."

My phone vibrated.

It was a text from Tanner: This is super boring, and that cologne is turning me on. Touch my private parts.

I responded: No, behave please. I have to get this deal done.

Tanner: He's not gonna budge, let's go to the bathroom and fuck. NEOW!

I shook my head no and sat my phone back on the table. Mayor Bierey was still blabbering.

It was obvious that the liquor was taking control of Tanner. She was trying to unbutton my pants under the table.

"Excuse me for a second Mr. Mayor, I need to have a word with my wife," I said, irritated.

Tanner and I stepped into the hallway that held the bathrooms and I whispered, "Go into that restroom and get yourself together, come back out with your business mentality on," I demanded as I turned and walked back to the dining table.

"I apologize for that, my wife has had a little too much to drink," I said apologetically.

"It's fine, my wife has the same problem, they probably should be in the ladies room together right now."

My attention was interrupted by a pair of thongs landing on my plate. I looked over and Tanner was laying back on the table across from us with her whole bottom half exposed.

I jumped up and ran to cover her up.

She started tugging at my belt.

"Tanner what the hell are you doing? I'm trying to conduct business here!" I whispered hard.

"Oh shut the fuck up, he's not going to let you have your compound in the hood. Since you wouldn't come to the bathroom and fuck me, we're doing it right here. Give it to me or I'll take it, your choice," she shrugged.

What the hell, she's right and I was not about to let her beat on me in front of the mayor. Not today. I allowed her to slide my pole inside of her.

The mayor gasped. "This is absurd and completely unacceptable. You will stop right this moment," he exclaimed.

Mrs. Bierey laughed. "Cap it Jon, you probably could learn a thing or two from them. I wish you were half as brave to do things like that."

I guess she ran their marriage too.

Tanner's moans brought the entire staff running to the dining area. They were all shocked at the scene that was unfolding in front of their eyes.

Meanwhile, I was just screwing my wife like we owned the place.

When I climaxed I didn't even say bye, I just threw $5000 on the table as we walked out of the restaurant.

Tanner sucked my dick in the elevator just so she could watch herself in the mirrored walls.

"We should put a camera system in the sex room so that I can go back and watch, this is turning me on," she said between pulls.

"Whatever you want, baby you got it," I moaned.

That night I kicked Day out of the room, I wanted Tanner all to myself so that I could give her all of me.

CHAPTER 57

My phone rang and woke me up at 7AM, I rolled over and grabbed it from the nightstand.

Unknown caller.

"Hello?" I answered, still half asleep.

"Mr. Khrist, how the hell are you?" asked the cheery caller.

"Sleep, other than that I'm fine. Who's this?" I asked as I sat up on the edge of the bed.

"What, you don't recognize my voice? It's Jon, Jon Bierey the mayor."

His tone didn't sound like the tone that came from the mayor that I met the previous night at all.

"My bad Mr. Bierey, I had a long night after we left the restaurant. Normally I'm an early riser but today I decided to catch up on some sleep. What can I do for you?"

"Oh I'm sure I know exactly what you mean. Say, do you have some time to come down to the old Vess factory by ten this morning to feed the homeless with me?"

I looked at the phone in disbelief, did he ask the thug that he wouldn't be seen doing business with to help him feed the homeless? In public?

"Sure I can make it, what's the catch?"

He laughed. "There's no catch, I'll wait for your arrival before I get started," he said before he hung up.

Tanner rolled over and saw that I was still staring at the phone. "What's the matter babe?"

"The mayor wants me to meet him downtown and help him feed the homeless. After last night I was sure that we put a fork in that coffin," I responded, still baffled.

"Maybe he was to have you arrested for public indecent exposure and he's luring you down there to do it," she suggested.

"Well I'm going to go anyway, make sure you have bail money pulled from the account just in case."

I got up and hit the shower.

Showered and dressed I walked into the kitchen. Day was naked and cooking breakfast while Tanner sat at the island scrolling through social media, per usual.

I gave Day a kiss on the forehead and went to sit down at the island next to Tanner.

Tanner looked up from her phone. "Where do you think you're going dressed like that?"

I looked down. "What's wrong with athletic wear?"

"You're meeting with the mayor, Husband. I'm sure they'll have cameras around, go change!" Tanner demanded.

"Why should I? He already thinks I'm a thug anyway and I'm probably about to go to jail behind your antics."

Tanner stood up out of her seat and pulled me out of mine, she pushed me upstairs to the bedroom.

Twenty minutes later I had on a black cashmere turtleneck sweater, black fitted slacks and Ferragamo loafers with the matching belt. The last detail was a gold faced Richard Mille that the girls bought me for Valentines Day.

She walked in a circle around me. "Now you'll look good in your mugshot, I still feel like something's missing," she said as she put her hand on her chin.

She thought for a minute then she went into my closet and brought out a gray peacoat. "Perfect, you look like you belong in pictures with the mayor. I'll call Big Chris and see if he's free."

What would I do without my wife?

Ten o'clock sharp my loafers were stepping out of the back of Big Chris's S63 Mercedes Benz.

Mayor Bierey was already on the scene shaking hands and talking to the homeless.

He turned to me with a smile as I approached. "The man of the hour. Ladies and gentlemen, meet Mr. Khrist."

I waved to the crowd and then the mayor and I posed for a round of photos. We fed and ate IMO's pizza with the vagrants of downtown's vagabond city.

An hour later the mayor and I were walking the bike trail that went through the abandoned factory district on the riverfront, which housed more vagrants. We shook their hands and gave the ones with children a few dollars and snapped pictures.

"Mr Mayor, after our dinner I left with the impression that you didn't do business with my kind, and now we're in public being seen together and taking pictures. To what do I owe the pleasure?"

He stopped walking and had a seat on a concrete divider.

"First, I want you to know that you and your wife's actions were undeniably distasteful and inexplicable..."

I stopped him in his tracks. "Mayor, you didn't have to call me all the way

388

down here to tell me your disgust. Also, you can insult me but I don't give a flying fuck who you are, you're not going to insult my wife," I said angrily.

He held his hand up. "That's not my intention, Khrist. If I'm going to do business with you then I have to clean up your image a little. That's why we're here today feeding the homeless and taking pictures," he explained in a softer tone.

I should have apologized to Dwayne 'The Rock' Johnson for stealing his eyebrow move for that one.

"Business? You just told me that business with me would not only make you look bad, but the city as a whole. Then you expressed your disgust about my wife's actions following dinner."

"I want you to listen to me. For the last twenty years of my marriage, Gabby and I have not been intimate in any way shape or form. It was so bad that we now sleep in separate rooms. Last night Gabby was so turned on by the performance that you and Tanner put on that after you left we had our own little action on the same table. At three o'clock in the morning I woke up in the backseat of my car, still parked in the garage of Kemoll's. We were so exhausted that we couldn't drive home after having more sex in the garage. By the time we made it home we had enough rest to work the rust off of the old sack. For the first time in fifteen years, my wife and I slept in the same bed.

So after we're done here, go home and thank your wife. You two sparked a well that dried up twenty years ago and brought life back into it. I can't wait to see the feats that we'll be able to accomplish together in the near future. Gabby was right, I need your electrifying persona around to drive this city back to euphoria. In doing so, my first objective and olive branch is to allow you to proceed with the land development that you explained last night."

I couldn't believe my ears nor did I know that I was staring.

The mayor shook my shoulder. "You still with me kid? Close your mouth, there's no telling what's floating in the air down here."

"I apologize sir, I just find it hard to believe that a display of fornication during a business meeting would be what landed this approval."

"Amongst other things, I think you have the talent and vision to be a positive figure in this community. You'll be able to reach those who are often forgotten or looked over. I'm anxious to hear what else you've got in that valedictorian brain of yours."

So he really did dig into my background, I thought to myself.

The mayor had a telephone, fax machine and a printer/scanner inside his mayoral limousine. He called his secretary and asked her to send over the necessary approval documents.

We signed the documents and faxed them back to his office and Darius, the land developer.

CHAPTER 58

After Big Chris dropped me off at home I told Tanner about the meeting.

"See, sex heals all. I'm so proud of you. Whatever you set your sights on, you always hit your mark. Now aren't you glad that you listened to me and changed your outfit this morning?" Tanner asked as she sat on my lap.

"No, but I am glad that you had the guts to seduce me in front of the mayor. I owe it all to you. I love you, without you I would be nothing." I said as I kissed her.

"You're everything without me, I'm only an emphasis to your greatness. Besides, I jacked you off at the dinner table with my parents sitting across from us, who the hell are those people? When mama wants some lovin' mama's going to get her lovin'. Understood?"

"Understood."

Darius was working on the developmental side of the project. The demolition of the area would start in a month.

I had to come up with a plan to get the area vacated so that we could proceed with construction. Luckily I was a quick thinker because the meeting rolled up on me fast.

I sent Billi up first to give me a few minutes to gather my thoughts. She went through the weekly numbers and updates. The few days we were gone didn't affect us financially because we fronted enough product to cover our absence and the businesses were run by managers daily anyway so our absence wasn't felt there.

She finished her weekly spiel with talk about investments then she turned it over to me.

"As you all know, the heat has been coming down pretty hard on the hood as of late. Chief Williams has brought it to my attention that government forces have been making inquiries about the Ashland neighborhood. How we got on the radar, I'm not sure but I think it's time that we vacate the area for about a year. I had a conversation with the mayor this morning and he's gotten the same news as well. The city is pushing to condemn the area from Taylor and Natural Bridge up to Newstead and Elmbank. Starting in a month the bulldozers will start on the vacos and spread from there. When and if we rebuild, we'll use shell companies to buy back." I lied. They say it's okay to stretch the truth when you're giving a surprise, right?

Deuce asked, "Isn't that shit illegal? What about everybody that's still living down there?"

"Thirty days' notice to vacate is all they have to give legally. Our families can live with us or they can take the thirty thousand that we offer everyone else to find new residences. The mayor says if the habitants of a house don't want to move then they'll return home to a crumbled building, so he's giving us the option to help the current occupants relocate. I know that's the only home we've known but we can't take on the U.S. government," I said, feeling the lie bumps forming on my tongue as I spoke.

Big Money asked, "Can't Knuckles help us? He's a part of the government."

"He's a general in the military, you think he'll stick his neck out for this and possibly tie himself to a crime organization?"

"I guess that makes sense, but how will we get everybody out?" he responded.

"We'll go door to door if we have to and give them the offer, it'll be better coming from us. Besides, I'm sure the letters and signs will be coming soon," I told the group.

At least now they will since I thought of it.

They took the news better than expected and I cut the meeting short. There was no need to keep them there after having a bomb dropped on their laps like that.

I couldn't find Tanner anywhere. Her phone was in the kitchen and her car was still in the garage. She wasn't in any of her normal areas, her dressing room, bedroom or the kitchen.

One last room to check before I started to panic. I opened the door to the sex room and the sight blew my mind. Tanner had Day strapped to the wall upside down and spread eagle. Tanner was standing and they were locked in a standing 69 position.

How the hell did Day get on the wall in that position? Head scratcher.

Tanner heard the door. "Your meeting is over quite early today. Wanna join us?" she asked.

I was still scratching my head. "As much as I would love to, I'm going to have to decline. I need your help with something. Is this what y'all do while I'm downstairs having my meetings?"

"Not all the time, sometimes I put on the strap-on and nail her in the asshole until she screams," Tanner smart ass said.

"I'm glad that our meetings are two floors down. I need your help with something important, babe."

"Okay, let me just bust my nut over this bitch's face and I'll be right with you. Are you sure you don't want to join first?" she asked as she started back humping Day in the face.

"No boo, business calls. I'll be downstairs."

Tanner walked into the living room naked and looked like she was exhausted.

"You look like you just got hit by a train and you need a nap," I said to her.

"Squirting really takes a lot out of you. What's up, what do you need help with?" she asked as she mounted me while I laid on the couch.

I had a hard time keeping my composure, I couldn't let her know that she was exciting me.

"You still know how to hack? Where the hell is Day?" I asked hoping that she wasn't still tied up.

"The hoe is sleeping. You wanna fuck?"

"What, no, stay on topic."

"I am on top of it, I can feel him too."

"Tanner, stop it, I'm being serious. Can you hack the newspaper before it prints tomorrow?"

"Ew, newspapers are so geriatric. Why would you want to hack them? Nobody reads newspapers but old people. You sure you don't want to fuck?"

"No, I mean yes! Yes I'm sure I don't want to right now. Anyway, I'm trying to reach the elderly anyway. The mayor is going to run our photo op of feeding the homeless, I need you to add that the neighborhood is going to be demolished for redevelopment in thirty days."

"Why can't you just tell them?"

"Stop touching that! I will tell them but I need the newspaper to back the story. You know old people are stubborn. I don't want them to know that I'm behind the development until the day of the ribbon cutting."

"Don't tell me not to touch what belongs to me. Yea I'll do it."

"It's attached to my body so that makes it mine. If you do a really good job, I might have to give Niema a call for you and Day. I'll even let y'all go alone with the business expenses card."

She jumped her naked ass off of me and ran to the man cave/office so fast.

Women are so easy.

The story ran Monday morning and I hit the streets going door to door. Majority of the habitants agreed with moving as long as they got the $30,000. A few were a little harder but when they realized that if they didn't take the thirty then they

would be broke and without a home.
By Friday everyone had agreed.

Darius understood the need to be
discreet and he agreed to build the
wall first after the demolition job. The
demolition commenced a month
later.

CHAPTER 59

Over the course of the previous eighteen months business skyrocketed across the board. Luh Borey dropped his album titled Traphouses and Ceiling Fans, Fatt Rell dropped his titles Food, both were touring across the country and constantly booked. Big Money's dealership was slanging cars like $5 chicken boxes, for Christmas he gifted the whole gang with Hellcats or Trackhawks. Jizzle signed two new artists to the label, Luh Iraq and Foeside Johnny, their buzz was taking off. Peezy was now selling houses to the millionaires, with commission alone he was able to live a luxurious lifestyle. Fox's transportation had a fleet of sixteen trucks and trailers, neither sat still longer than the required break period of ten hours. Reddot's Dirty Angels was now the it-spot to be when the sun went to sleep.

Business on the other side was doing spectacular as well. So well that Knuckles decided to buy out the private airstrip so that our shipments could land on our command. The weekly disbursements were up to $7,000,000 a piece, everybody did their share and everybody ate.

The Bierey's became real close to my family. At first it blew their minds about our situation with Day but they eventually warmed up to it and got their own sex slave for their marriage. They came over weekly and when they felt like it, they utilized the sex room. Tanner taught Gabby how to squirt and I gave Jon some pointers on how to be rough but pleasurable. Together we taught them how to be spontaneous. I hooked them up with Mike down on South Beach and they went down to experience the sky diving sex box.

It wasn't always about sex though. Jon and I discussed issues on our respective sides of the law. The suggestions that I suggested were;

help the lower class more, give more options to enjoy the city, police officers that had complaints of abuse were to be fired and lastly the officers must reside in the district that they're policing. It'll be hard to abuse a citizen when they know where you laid your head. His suggestions to me were; guide the youth to a better future than the street life, open after school programs to keep the kids occupied and to interact with the community more positively. He also suggested adding a park and pool within the walls of Ashland Ave.

It's amazing the concepts that two people from two different walks of life can come up with when they listen to each other.

CHAPTER 60

Everyday since the wall went up the whole gang and elders kept asking what they were doing on the inside, I would just shrug my shoulders. Then the answers were starting to be demanded when the high rise peaked the height of the wall. I couldn't count the amount of lies that I had to come up with to keep them off of my back. I was ecstatic when the day came that I didn't have to lie anymore.

I sent out a text to the AAG group chat: Grab your families and meet me on Elmbank where the church used to be.

The ribbon cutting day had finally arrived.

Tanner dressed me to match her and Day's dresses for the occasion. She knew the cameras would eat that up during the press conference.

Knuckles, The Biereys, Chief Williams and the whole AAG attended the ceremony.

Jon gave a brief speech on how he wished us nothing but the best and how he wanted to work with us to do more developmental projects throughout the city.

It was my time to shine. "For the last eighteen months I've had to do one of the hardest things that I've ever had to do, and that was having to lie to y'all so that I could secretly build this place of euphoria for you all. The obstacles we've overcome and the success that we've had, I owe it all to y'all. In return, I've taken some resources available to me to give you all this town within a town. I know y'all looked at me crazy when I knocked on your doors but after you all took my word, I was able to give us our own unique gated community. It's our turn to show the world what a few guys out of the trenches can do with hard work and dedication," Tanner and I cut the ribbon then I continued, "I give you the Compound at Ashland Ave."

They all shouted "A's up or K's up till my days up!"

Yeah, I'm almost certain that the news channels will edit that part out.

I showed them the way to access the garage. We came above ground through the high rise access. The gang picked their houses as we walked the grounds and our families chose their floors in the condos.

The festivities only lasted an hour. Tanner, Day and I were in the foyer of our mini mansion.

She said, "You know, I don't want to get rid of the house in Barrington Downs. It has too many of our first memories and if we ever need to get away, we'll always have a place to escape to."

"If that's what my wife wants, then I guess it's my job to grant that wish."

"How about all three of us bless this house before we move in? It might take a while longer because there's more rooms here than in the Downs," Tanner suggested.

We closed the door and had our sex triangle in every room in the house. If the electricity would have been connected, we would have stayed all night.

As we were walking out of the garage of the compound Tanner turned and looked back.

"What's bothering you, babe?"

"I can't help but to think that we should do a house for Banga and start an honor wall right outside of the garage entrance, kind of like they did for the Vietnam vets in Washington."

"You know what, that's a great idea. You complete me my love," I said as we continued to the G-Wagon.

CHAPTER 61

They say time flies when you're having fun and in my experience that's true.

Five years had passed since the opening of the compound. It worked wonders, we hadn't had any incidents or any faults. No unwanted company could breach a thirty foot wall so when we wanted, we could hang out on the block without having to worry about bullets or handcuffs.

Mayor Bierey earned a third term with me as his token black guy, which kept the heat off of our operation.

All of the OGs of Ashland which were our families took quarters in the high rise. Each condo held five rooms and three bathrooms so that everybody was able to live comfortably and rent free.

Tanner, Day and I were still rolling in full effect. We even built a new and improved sex room in the mansion.

Life couldn't be any better.

One morning the three of us went to eat breakfast at a new spot called Freddie G's. I had to handle some business afterwards so Tanner drove her Audi RS7 that she got for her birthday the prior year, I followed them in my new Dodge Ram Mammoth.

"Baby, the Audi needs an oil change, brakes and tires for the winter. When will you have time to get it to the shop?"

"I'll do it today, I can drop it off at I-70 Performance and have Ickey or Donnie take me to the warehouse. Y'all can take the Beast while they fix it," I said.

Responsibilities of a husband.

"You know I hate driving that big dumb ass truck," Tanner said frowning.

"Okay, well we'll drop your car off at the shop and then y'all Uber home."

"Fine, I'll drive the big stupid Beast," she said while pouting and crossing her arms.

"How about you ladies go and have a spa and nails day then? Would that make driving the Beast worth your while?"

Damage Control always seemed to help cheer her up.

Tanner's spending habits were outrageous so I had to make an account just for her shopping and pampering excursions.

"Okay, I'm putting ten grand in the self care account. Go and enjoy yourselves."

We finished up our meals and headed out to the vehicles. I walked them to the Beast and gave both of them kisses. For some reason I felt that was okay to do to Day, it was the first time ever. I even told her that I loved her for the first time.

I got into the Audi and got behind the Beast so that I could trail them, we got caught at the light. Time slowed down to a crawl and my breathing got heavy. I started looking around at my surroundings, something had caught my attention.

A black Charger was creeping up the shoulder of the road.

I pulled my ARP up and aimed it at the passenger door at the ready but then I remembered that I was in Tanner's car, I relaxed as they passed me. I kept my eyes trained on them, just in case.

Then the Beast came into my peripheral vision, it dawned on me that they knew my truck and Tanner was in it at that moment, right in front of me.

But it was too late , by the time I got out of the car and to the passenger side of the Beast three shots had already been sent into the truck.

I started shooting at the Charger when the back window shattered, I saw that I had hit someone in the backseat, their head was leaning on the headrest of the driver seat.

I got off a total of five shots before the driver sped off. I gave chase on foot until I realized that I was only wasting bullets.

I turned and took off running back to my truck.

Day was laying over the driver seat when I slung the passenger door open. I started panicking then I saw Day move.

Tanner was pushing Day off of her. Day didn't have a pulse when I checked.

Tanner broke down in my arms. "She sacrificed herself to save my life. Her last words were, I couldn't let them take you from Daddy, he would suffer without you. Baby, Day put her life on the line to preserve our happiness. Since we pulled off all she talked about was you telling her that you loved her," she sobbed.

By that time, I was holding Tanner close to my heart. I couldn't find any words to say. What I do know is I'll be suffering without Day too. I lost one of my wives that day. I broke down and started bawling with Tanner in my arms.

I owed it to Day to even the score and maybe even more. It was time to get in demon mode.

"How do you want to do this G.I.?" Shoota asked.

We were watching the drone feed on my laptop in the alley of Lex Ave, we were about to catch our cuts.

"We hit them from eight different gangways, two people in each cut. We don't leave until there's no one left standing. I'll hit the cut and count to thirty then I'll light a pack of Black Cats and throw them behind them. That's going to divert their attention then we pop out and fire their asses up," I directed looking up from the screen.

Lazy asked, "What if it's women out there?"

What happened with Day turned my heart cold. "They started that game. I wanna make them muhfuckas feel exactly how I feel, ain't nobody spared!"

Eyes started smiling. "You ain't said nothing but a word."

I brought the drone back and loaded it into the car before I could change my mind then we caught our cuts.

I waited thirty seconds to make sure everybody was in position, then I launched the fireworks on the other side of the crowd.

Someone saw me but before they had the chance to react, the Black Cats started popping and they all turned toward the noise.

Then the massacre started.

We were shooting and they were running but everywhere that they were trying to run to, one of us was there to light them up. We turned them every way except lose, demon mode was in full effect.

When we got done there were eleven still bodies laying on the street. We even set the black Charger on fire.

Somehow, I still felt empty, I had to feed that hunger. I threw a grenade through the window of their hangout house when it detonated I heard screams from inside. It took everything in me to contain myself from running in and smoking everybody in that bitch.

The next morning the news covered the slaughter, in total there were thirteen fatalities and seven severely injured. Thanks to Chief Williams, it was chocked up to their hood turning on each other after a fight broke out.

Tanner hadn't left the bed since the day of Day's death, I can't say that I blamed her. Our world had crumbled before our eyes.

Day's funeral was a week later. Shoota stood next to me for support as I stood over the hole they lowered her casket into.

Looking into the hole I said, "I can't do this shit no more, gang. I lost a part of my life and it could have easily been the both of them. This shit touched my wife dawg! I, I have to walk away while I still can, gang."

"What about the business?" He asked.

"We all have more than enough money to live comfortably. I suggest those that are on the drug side invest in something to their particular talent. We'll still be able to eat off of the legal side until they get up and running. I can't take anymore losses, Day's death is on my hands. Even though Tanner won't admit it, she knows that it's my fault."

I started crying the hardest any of my guys have ever seen. I felt all of their hands touch me at once.

Sanchez said, "We got you G.I. Joe."

My AAG brothers held me up because my world no longer had a surface for me to stand on.

CHAPTER 62

Knuckles understood where I was coming from and decided that we'd made more than enough money that our great great great grandkids would still be rich. The city would have to find new suppliers.

The crew was okay with the decision as well. Nobody wanted to lose anymore of the home team.

Knuckles helped them find locations for their new businesses.

Relex went into the electrical field, Deuce went into the professional drag racing field, Sanchez opened up a high end retail shop, Animal opened up a barbershop for celebrities, Eyes and Stuck both started taking professional murder for hire jobs and Shoota opened a gun store with an indoor shooting range.

The cats from the Lex disappeared all together.

As for me and Tanner, we moved to South Beach, Florida. She finally wanted to sell the Barrington Downs house because it had too many memories of Day. I talked her out of selling the Ashland Ave mansion so that if we went to town we would have somewhere safe to stay.

We opened a sex studio and named it Sexercise. Three times a day we held a class for an hour, we taught positions, toys, film, the whole nine. We also learned more as well. If we saw couples performing a position that we haven't tried, we tried it ourselves. It's incredible how comfortable strangers can be while having sex in a room full of other strangers having sex. We had our regulars and we had tourists. Mayor Bierey and Gabby visited our class twice a year. Mike and his wife came through from time to time.

Although Day's death took a toll on us, we were finally happy again.

"Who would have ever thought that we would be doing the very thing that we cherish the most for a living?" I asked Tanner.

"And what's that?"

"Each other."

"You're trying to talk me out of my panties again?" she asked, then she eyed me.

"Does it come with a happy ending?"

"Always."

"Then yes, because you are my happy ending."

I kissed my wife and made love to her like no time before. She cried because it was so sensual.

We were living the life again.

Get in, run it up and get out.
A's up or K's up till my days up!

Made in the USA
Monee, IL
25 March 2025

14600180R00246